MARGARET MACDONELL is Chairman of the Department of
Celtic Studies at St Francis Xavier University, Nova Scotia.

Every man has a story to tell and this was no less true of the
hundreds of emigrants from the Highlands and Hebrides who
crossed the Atlantic from the late eighteenth century to the
early twentieth century to settle in North America.

This selection of Scottish Gaelic songs brings to light the
revealing and often touching poems of some twenty such emigrants. Focusing on themes of emigration and exile, their sub-
jects range from the biblical motif of liberation from tyranny
(predestined by the Creator who provided a land of bounty
across the seas), to the happier future anticipated for his
daughter by a loyalist fugitive in North Carolina; from a
sense of security on the part of a clergyman settled in Pictou
County after the disruption in his homeland, to the disenchantment of an emigrant to Manitoba who longed to move
on to North Dakota. Their tone may be lyrical, elegaic, or
satirical.

Songs from various parts of the new world – the Carolinas,
Nova Scotia, Prince Edward Island, Ontario, and the Canadian
west – are included in Gaelic with a facing English translation.
A short biography of each bard prefaces the selections attributed to him or her. Detailed notes provide a guide to sources
and variant texts, elucidate obscure passages, and define the
social and cultural context in which the songs originated.

This is a book that will inform and entertain both the spe-
cialist and the general reader.

MARGARET MACDONELL

The Emigrant Experience: Songs of Highland Emigrants in North America

UNIVERSITY OF TORONTO PRESS
TORONTO BUFFALO LONDON

Canadian Cataloguing in Publication Data

MacDonell, Margaret, 1920-
  The emigrant experience
  Songs in Gaelic with English translations.
  Includes index.
  Bibliography
  ISBN 0-8020-5469-2 (bound) ISBN 0-8020-6489-2 (pbk.)
  1. Folk-songs, Gaelic – Canada – Texts. 2. Folk-songs,
Gaelic – United States – Texts. 3. Folk-songs, Gaelic
– Canada – Translations into English. 4. Folk-songs,
Gaelic – United States – Translations into English.
5. Gaels in Canada – Songs and music. 6. Gaels in
United States – Songs and music. I. Title.
PB1684.M32   891.631'040897   C81-094021-3

Contents

Càirdean nan Gàidheal le fonn
Tha nis air am bonn 's gach àit';
Cothrom gu fhaotainn do'n t-sluagh
An deas agus tuath gun dàil.

DUNCAN BLACK BLAIR

Gaelic clansmen of courage
now dwell in every land
where opportunity awaits them
without delay, to the south and to the north.

Preface

The texts of the songs edited in this work reflect a chapter of Highland history whose consequences affected the destiny of thousands of Gaels both at home and far beyond the seas. The significance of Scottish Gaelic songs of emigration was first brought to my attention by Charles W. Dunn, Margaret Brooks Robinson, Professor of Celtic Languages and Literatures, Harvard University, under whose gracious direction I was led to explore this vast and varied repertoire. I acknowledge with deep gratitude his many kindnesses, including permission to transcribe from his personal recordings the text of the song *Tha mise fo ghruaimean*.

To my father and mother I owe the gift of my native language. To my constant friend and former professor, Sister Mairi Mac-Donald (Sister St Veronica) CND, my debt is incalculable. Many others gave generous assistance and numerous courtesies: the Congregation de Notre Dame, released time for graduate study; the president and administration of St Francis Xavier University, tuition fellowship for Celtic studies, and the University Council for Research, grant for the preparation of the manuscript for publication; the Canada Council, two-year doctoral fellowship; Harvard University, travelling fellowship; the librarians at St Francis Xavier University, Harvard, the National Library of Scotland, the School of Scottish Studies of Edinburgh University, and the James McConnell Memorial Library, Sydney, Nova Scotia. To all, my warmest thanks.

For permission to use texts and/or quotations, as recorded in the notes, I am grateful to Donald Gillis, editor of *The Casket*; Professor Derick C. Thomson, editor of *Gairm*; John Lorne Campbell of Canna; John Donald Publishers Ltd, Edinburgh; Hugh Barron, Honorary Secretary of the Celtic Society of Inverness. My thanks also to the Reverend James MacKenzie, Olivia, North Carolina; the Reverend D.M. Sinclair, Halifax; the late Professor C.I.N. MacLeod, Antigonish; Harry Baglole, editor of the *Island Magazine*, Charlottetown; Hugh MacMillan, Department of Public Records and Archives, Toronto; Robert L. Fraser, manuscript editor, Dictionary of Canadian Biography; Professor J.M. Bumsted, Simon Fraser University; Mrs J. Beryl Barrett, Charlottetown; and Ms Prudence Tracy, editor, University of Toronto Press; all of whom gave assistance of various kinds. Finally, sincere thanks to Donald Meek, University of Glasgow, and John Shaw, Research Associate, St Francis Xavier University, who read the manuscript and made many helpful corrections and suggestions.

Publication of this book is made possible by a grant from the Canadian Federation for the Humanities, using funds provided by the Social Sciences and Humanities Research Council of Canada, and a grant to the University of Toronto Press from the Andrew W. Mellon Foundation.

MARGARET MacDONELL
Saint Francis Xavier University
July 1979

THE BARDS AND THEIR SONGS

Introduction

Some years ago John Lorne Campbell of Canna pointed out convincingly that the Highland attitude towards the Jacobite Rising of 1745 found authentic expression in the Gaelic songs and poetry of the people most directly affected by it.[1] In many respects the same holds true of the massive exodus from the Highlands and Islands of Scotland, which began in the 1770s and lasted well over a century. This movement elicited an extensive repertoire of songs in which its tragic aspects received due notice, but not to the exclusion of other considerations. The bards, many of them emigrants, usually tempered their compositions with a note of optimism as they looked to a more prosperous and secure life abroad. They were careful to record many of the factors incident to emigration and did so with remarkable accuracy, so much so that many of their songs are an illuminating supplement to contemporary sources as well as to later historical studies.

A small number of these songs allude to the old order and express a yearning for its restoration, and particularly for the security which the clan system provided for its members. Occasionally a reference to the stories and songs enjoyed in the good company of old bears on the ancient literary tradition, which was fostered and sustained by the old order. Deep in that tradition were vestiges of poetry akin to emigrant songs. In the ancient tale that bears her name, Deirdre left Scotland with heavy heart. She wept, and then she sang:

Is ionmhuinn an tìr, an tìr ud thall,
Albainn choillteach, lingeantach;
Is goirt le m' chridhe bhi 'gad fhàgail,
Ach tha mi 'falbh le Naois.[2]

Fair is the land, the land yonder,
wooded, lake-filled Scotland;
sore is my heart at leaving it,
but I am going with Naois.

In a twelfth-century poem, one of many ascribed to St Columba, the celebrated *peregrinus* took delight in climbing to the top of Uchd Ailuin in Iona, so that he 'might often see there the calm of the sea ... and hear the sound of the shallow waves against the rocks.'[3] There he wished his mystical name to be Cùl ri Erinn (Back turned to Ireland). Exile grieved him, but he rejoiced that it moved him to contrition and contemplation.

Since Highland emigrant songs were a direct consequence of the disintegration of the clan system and the evolution of a new social order, they can best be understood in the context of these developments. For centuries prior to the '45, the Gàidhealtachd (Gaelic area) of Scotland was subject to patriarchal government by devotion, consent, and obligation. The land upon which the clan resided belonged not to the chief but to the entire clan, members of which were proud, independent, and integral to the system. Land was held not directly from the chief but from the tacksman, usually a close relative or member of the chief's family. Estates were fairly extensive but economically backward with their multiple tacks on which tenants eked out a subsistence living. But loyalties were strong, and clan bards elegized and eulogized their chiefs and praised their numerous retainers for their prowess in battle. Such in very brief outline was the system which was destroyed after the defeat of the Jacobite army at Culloden in 1746.[4]

That this system was an anachronism, not only in Britain but in western Europe, has been convincingly demonstrated by James Hunter in his recent definitive study of the crofting community.[5] At a time when 'improvement' of agrarian areas kept pace more or less with the rapid commercial expansion rampant in southern Britain, Highland chiefs were faced with an obvious dilemma: either the clan system must yield radically to the trends of the times or endure in the face of them. Reconciliation of these alternatives was clearly impossible, for, as Hunter points out, 'The essential feature of that system was that it depended on land being laid out to ensure the continued existence of the clan system as a socially unified and militarily effective organization, considerations of agricultural efficiency being of decidedly secondary importance.'[6] Thus, whatever their personal inclination or cupidity might dictate, chiefs felt constrained to favour, at least ostensibly, the dictates of a system ill-suited to improvement in the form of money rents and a drastic reduction of tenancies. Happily for them, though not for their kin, the resolution of their dilemma was effected by political and strategic, rather than economic or social considerations.

Throughout the first half of the eighteenth century Highland Jacobitism posed a serious threat to the British government. The '45, like the earlier risings of 1715 and 1719, demonstrated that the predominant sentiments in many parts of Gaeldom at the time were 'a passionate attachment for the *de jure* royal House, coupled with a bitter hatred for the usurping dynasty'[7] and utter contempt for the foe. It was to clansmen that the great Mac Mhaighstir Alasdair (Alexander MacDonald) addressed his stirring incitement, for the clan was the nursery of these sentiments:

O!·chlanna bha bras
Riamh nach robh tais,
    Am maith sibh do *rascalaibh* bùirt oirbh?
Fhineachan gasd'
Cruinnichibh cas,
    'S faigh'maid air n-ais ar n-ainm cliùiteach.
Cha n-eil am Breatunn de chuideachd

Na chuireas ruinn cluigean,
  Ach deanadh a'bhuidrisg ar dùsgadh,
Na tha'Ghàidhealaibh arrant'
Eadar Gallaibh us Arainn,
  'S na tha *Jacobites* Gallach 's gach dùthaich.

O! valorous clans
Who never showed fear,
  Will you suffer that rascals should mock you?
O splendid tribes
Gather up quick,
  To win back our name that was famous;
No company in Britain
Can ever resist us.
  When once our fierce wrath has aroused us,
All the proud Gaels
From Caithness to Arran,
  And the Jacobites from the Low Countries.[8]

Culloden, then, was but the prelude to a thoroughgoing eradica-
tion of the system whose members were wont to respond with
alarming alacrity to such a call. As Hunter points out, the battle
itself was not only a catastrophic defeat for Highland arms, it
was much more:

What distinguished Culloden from previous reverses ... was the fact
that it was merely an overture to a massive assault on the social and
political institutions of clanship. In 1746 and in the years that followed
clansmen – Jacobite and non-Jacobite – were disarmed finally and completely, the wearing of the Highland dress was prohibited, and the
chiefs' judicial powers over their clans were abolished – developments
that were accompanied by a determined effort to modernize the Highland economy and to *integrate* the region and its people into a civiliza-
tion from which they had hitherto kept aloof.[9]

Integration procedures took many forms: the widespread destruction of Highland homes, the execution of many Jacobite
supporters, the annexation of forfeited estates to the crown in

1752, and the abolition of hereditary jurisdictions in 1754. For over forty years the forfeited estates were administered by government commissioners, who introduced changes in landholding and agriculture. Under their direction tenants were granted leases for fixed periods, and only single holdings were permitted. This arrangement ruled out subletting and, of course, excluded the tacksman.[10] In 1784 practically all the chiefs (or their families) had recovered their estates, and there is ample evidence that by then 'any lingering traces of a patriarchal outlook had been strictly subordinated to the pursuit of profit, and Highland "chieftains" were firmly set on the road to becoming the landed and anglicized gentlemen that they have ever since remained.'[11] In time the surrender of hereditary jurisdictions had been compensated by a payment of £152,000 to the chiefs, and much of this money was diverted to the 'improvement' of their estates. Turning these remote and crowded estates to best advantage was not an easy task for the chiefs themselves; for their kinsfolk it was a source of incalculable misery and distress. Thus, painfully, the old order passed and with it the traditional bonds of kinship and affection between chief and clan, while in its wake the new order gave rise on an unprecedented scale to evictions, exploitation, and emigration.

How and to what extent did this radical reorganization of Highland society induce large numbers of Gaels to leave the country and seek their fortune elsewhere? Answers to these questions vary widely, and obviously a detailed analysis of them is beyond the scope of this work.[12] But, as already stated, the simple poetic observations of the people most directly affected constitute an independent source of information and are of great value and interest. Highland emigrant songs abound with references to 1/ increased rents, 2/ the introduction of sheep, 3/ the new landlords and their functionaries, and 4/ the general disregard for tenantry and retainers, thus reflecting conditions which made emigration inevitable and irresistible to thousands of Highlanders.

1/ Bards' complaints about increased rents can be amply substantiated from records dating as far back as 1750.[13] In Assynt rents rose from £555.0.5 in 1757 to £654.4.5 in 1766.[14] In North

Uist they went from £1200 in 1763 to £1800 in 1777. By 1785 Glenorchy rents had risen by 200 to 300 per cent, and in the Hebrides they had increased five-fold by 1811.[15] Almost to a man, passengers on board the *Bachelor*, emigrating from Caithness and Sutherland to North Carolina in 1773, named high rents as the principal reason for leaving the homeland.[16] Since cattle were the chief source of revenue with which tenants could meet their rental payments, a disaster like the cattle plague of 1771 posed insurmountable problems for them. Worse still were the adverse effects on cattle grazing incident to the coming of sheep as part of the program of modernization of the estates at the turn of the century.

2/ Gaelic bards leave little doubt as to the unhappy relation between emigration and the introduction of sheep into the Highlands. The subject has been controverted assiduously by scholars over the years, and a brief look at opposing views is pertinent here.[17] In 1806 Robert Brown addressed strong criticisms to the earl of Selkirk, following the publication of Selkirk's *Observations* on conditions in the Highlands.[18] Brown rejected the earl's contention that sheep farming was a direct cause of emigration, citing Argyll as an area from which hundreds had emigrated long before the introduction of sheep. Margaret I. Adam, writing in 1920, admitted that sheep farming did displace population and thus contributed to emigration, but she hastened to add that the extent of the displacement had been exaggerated.[19]

As agent for Clanranald, Brown was concerned not only with sheep farming but also with the lucrative kelp industry introduced in 1765. While the run-rig system had been engulfed by the 'white tide' as clearances were ruthlessly extended, thousands of tenants faced the problem of relocation. But that they should leave the estates was unthinkable: they were essential to the 'dirty and disagreeable employment' required for the production of kelp. As the record shows, their relocation on small unproductive crofts not only assured the landlord an ample supply of labour, but set the stage for further exploitation in the usual form – an increase in rents. Even the Passenger Act of 1803, while ostensibly intended to regulate conditions on emigrant ships, was in reality designed to prevent the departure of these wretched people for America. So much for Brown. Adam's studies served as an introduction to the causes of Highland emigration, but her views, too, must now yield to the evidence so ably and convincingly adduced by Hunter.[20]

For over a century, of course, such moderate views have been flatly and unanimously refuted by Gaelic bards. They are equally unacceptable to present-day residents in many parts of the Highlands. The Gaels of Mallaig and Morar (to mention only one region) are not impressed by scholarly references to erroneous notions in folk memory about compulsion, evictions, and dispossession in time of the clearances.[21] One cannot but be moved, as I have been on several occasions, when these people point with a deep sense of tragedy to the craggy, deserted croftland rising from the Sound of Sleat, once the home of kinsfolk, who escaped extinction only by leaving the country. The ubiquitous bracken is another grim reminder of what sheep brought in their wake.

It is highly significant that a recent authority attributes 'the marked deterioration of the Gaelic culture ... in part to this tremendous social upheaval and misery caused by the incoming of the sheep and the mass movement of the populations of the glens.'[22] This statement accords well with an observation made by one of the later Gaelic bards in a song which alludes to emigration:

Cha b'ionadh ged a' bhàsaicheadh
An cànain milis màthaireil;
Cha labhair féidh nam fàsaichean
'S tha 'chaora bhàn gun chòmhradh.[23]

It is not surprising
that the sweet mother tongue should die;
the deer in the wilderness do not speak
and the white sheep has no language.

3/ That the new landlords and their functionaries served as a key factor in the general disruption following Culloden is clearly beyond dispute. But, like all generalizations, those pertaining to chiefs and lairds in the Highlands throughout the emigration period can be countered by exceptions, albeit in this case very few. The exactions of the laird of Boisdale, which led Captain John MacDonald of Glenaladale to remove Catholic tenants from South Uist to Prince Edward Island in 1772, support the view that the new lairds made life insufferable on their estates. But the circumstances attending that particular emigration did not necessarily obtain elsewhere in the Gàidhealtachd. Boisdale differed quite radically from his contemporary, MacLeod of Raasay, who hosted Boswell and Johnson during their tour of the Hebrides in 1773. Raasay received only about £250 to £300 rent from his estates, which included land in Rona and in Skye; yet he lived 'in great splendour and so far [was] he from distressing his people, that, in the present rage for emigration, not a man [had] left his estate.'[24] Raasay's benevolence was particularly impressive because it was exceptional. Certainly the early nineteenth-century clearances in Strathglass and Sutherland justified the cry of the Gaelic bards against the new lairds. A few decades later complaints were further justified by evictions such as those carried out by Colonel Gordon of Cluny in South Uist and Barra.[25]

Some of the unfavourable references to uachdaran (chief or overlord) in the emigrant songs may have been directed to the tacksmen. As already indicated, the reorganization of the forfeited estates by government commissioners tended to exclude the time-honoured office of these gentlemen. Consequently, when they found themselves reduced to the status of ordinary lessees, faced with the obligation of increased rents, many of them chose to leave the country, and they took their tenants with them.[26] In some respects the tacksmen were the natural leaders and proponents of emigration. Complaints about their complicity in the matter are recorded as far back as 1773. Captain Sutherland, general commissioner of the estates of Sutherland, expressed his apprehensions about one of them in a letter addressed to Alexander MacKenzie of Dunrobin in May of that year: 'All I shall observe on the list of Arrears is that Ken: Scobie has money to buy the imigrants cattle, which enables them to put their dreams about America in execution, yet he has not money to pay the Countess her Rent.'[27]

Not all tacksmen went to America, however, nor did they disappear entirely from the scene at home.[28] Presumably some of those who remained were kindly disposed toward their tenants, but for the most part their role and conduct had altered entirely. The change can be attributed in some measure to the after effects of the '45, although it had already begun before then in some parts of the Highlands.[29]

In the traditional military organization of the clans the tacksman had been an essential element. He paid for his tack by providing fighting men when they were needed, his money rent being merely nominal. The '45 saw the last of the old clan levies. Proprietors from then on looked upon their tacksmen as useless middlemen on poor, unproductive estates. Tacksmen were not good farmers, and they did little or nothing to modernize the lands they administered. Worse still they were not good masters. In addition to exacting high rents, they demanded exhaustive services from their tenants. In the Hebrides these could run to five days a week; in parts of Sutherland they were equally oppressive.[30] Their system of granting leases was indefinite and precarious in the extreme, especially for the poorer tenants. Yet, many of them remained in office well into the nineteenth century. Possibly proprietors were reluctant to dismiss them if they were close relatives. Perhaps they feared that leasing to lesser tenants would only compound the problems of inefficiency and lack of improvements on their estates.

In the eighteenth century the role of the factor was usually assumed by one of the gentlemen tacksmen. Records indicate that this official carried out his duties efficiently. He visited farms frequently, collected rents, observed the tenants at work, and encouraged their improvements. It is quite likely that, in addition to these duties, he was also baron-baillie, supervising and enforcing the tenants' duty to the laird. At least in some areas, the factor was a salaried official whose services drew from £12 to £33, depending on the size of the estates which he administered.[31] By the nineteenth century he was a very unpopular figure, if one is to judge by allusions in the songs of the emigrants.

4/ As observers of the havoc wrought by emigration, Gaelic bards were highly sensitive to the consequent fate of retainers, once the pride of their clan and the brave defenders of their country. Something of the old heroic ideal emerges as they sing about these gallant hosts who are rejected by the new lairds and even by their own families. Repeatedly the bards allude to the peril in which Britain now finds itself: if Napoleon should come the sheep who have replaced retainers will hardly be an adequate defence. This same theme is well known to readers of Sir Walter Scott; it also occurs in the familiar 'Canadian Boat Song.'[32]

In addition to these compelling negative factors, emigration received a positive impetus from letters and reports sent back to the old country by Highlanders who had already made their way to the New World.[33] In one of the oldest emigrant songs extant (ca 1774), John Macrae, the bard of Kintail, expresses his eagerness to get news from his friends who have gone to North Carolina:

B'fheàrr leam gu'n cluinninn uaibh sgeula,
Ciamar tha sibh 'n déidh na mara.

'M bith sibh 'g iarraidh tuilleadh chàirdean
Dh'fhios an àite d'rinn sibh fantainn?[34]

I wish I would get news from you
of how you are after your voyage.

Would you ask more of your friends
to come to the place where you are now settled?

In an even older song (ca 1771), Donald Matheson anticipates favourable reports from emigrants leaving Sutherland for the Carolinas.[35] Such communications were not always accurate accounts of what pioneer life was really like, as later emigrants affirmed in later songs.

Misconceptions about the New World did not derive exclusively from the letters of friends and relatives. Once emigration had become a business – and shipping companies especially regarded it as such from its inception – emigration agents combed the Highlands in search of prospective passengers and spared neither oratory nor trickery to achieve their ends. The blandishments of one of the most notorious of these, Archibald MacNiven, are implied in a news item reported in the *Caledonia Mercury* and copied later in Cape Breton. MacNiven's ships, described as clean and comfortable, were anchored at Snizort in Skye 'for the purpose of removing forever several hundred souls to Cape Breton and Prince Edward Island.' The report continues: 'The natives, sensible of the many disadvantages arising from a superabundant population to that of 1836 and 1837, have voluntarily resolved in great numbers to emigrate to Her Majesty's colonies in the already mentioned Islands.'[36]

Whether or not the seven hundred Skye residents who had so 'resolved' regretted the decision is unknown. The chagrin of Uist emigrants, who succumbed to MacNiven's wiles, is recorded in a song by an unidentified bard:

Muinntir Uidhist 'rinn an eucoir
Uile gu léir 'n uair a ghluais iad;
Thug iad an cuid do Mhac Naoimhein
Gus an cur a thìr an fhuachda.
Cha'n 'eil gnothach aig duin' aosd ann
Duine faoin cha dean e buannachd;
Ach luchd airgid 's gillean òga,
'S iad is dòcha deanamh suas ann.

Thug a' Muileach an car buileach
As a h-uile gin a spùill e;
Bha e fo 'n aois bha air liathadh
Le bhriagan a' tigh'nn do'n dùthaich.
Gur maith a dh'fhaodadh am Bàillidh
Fàbhur a dheanamh dhuinne,
Mur biodh gu'n d'rinn iad suas ris
Gus ar fuadach as an dùthaich.[37]

> The people of Uist made a mistake,
> all of them, when they moved;
> they gave their possessions to MacNiven
> to bring them out to the land of cold.
> No old person should go there;
> the ordinary man will not survive.
> Only well-to-do people and young men
> are likely to prosper there.

> The Mull man deceived completely
> every one he cheated.
> He had not yet turned grey
> when he came with his lies to our country.
> The Baillie could very well
> have done us a favour,
> if he had not conspired with him
> to lure us away from the country.

Such then were the reflections of Gaelic bards with respect to the causes and effects of emigration. Strangely enough the horrible shipping conditions, which practically all emigrants had to endure, receive no mention (to my knowledge) in any of their songs.[38] It will be seen below that songs about the trans-Atlantic voyage are usually cheery and spirited. The vessel is compared to a lively steed, ready to take to the waves with daring and vigour, a metaphor redolent of an interesting Norse tradition.[39] Songs which describe in some detail the hardships encountered on arrival in the New World make no reference to the misery of the long and ill-provisioned voyage there.

It is remarkable, too, that the notion of religious freedom as a desideratum for the emigrants does not occur in their songs. A favourite theme, recurring in various forms throughout the repertoire, is that of liberation from servility, comparable to the exodus from Egypt under Moses. Occasionally bards mention the need for divine assistance, either during the voyage or at the end of their long lives. Only in one song (among all those examined for this work) is there an exhortation and that to Catholics who left Strathglass about 1802.[40] Malcolm Ferguson, who emigrated from South Uist in 1843 and settled at Port

Morien, Cape Breton, described the religious harmony that pre-
vailed among the mixed groups with whom he sailed on the
Neith:

Bha sinn anns an t-soitheach ud cho mòr as gach aon dhe na h-eilea-
nan an iar, 's bha sinn de chaochladh eaglaisean, 's cha chualas facal a'
tighinn eadruinn fhad 's bha sinn còmhla.[41]

In that ship we were from all of the Western Islands, and from different
churches, but not a word of discord was heard among us while we were
together.

Almost all emigrant songs, even those which reveal the deep
sorrow of the emigrants on leaving home, evince a strong urge to
venture into a new and prosperous land and to enjoy the freedom and abundance to be found there. Certainly many Gaels left
the old country more through necessity than inclination. But
with the rapid rise in population in the latter part of the eighteenth century, it is reasonable to assume that many more did so
through ambition and the desire to become proprietors, away
from the congested holdings and exorbitant rents known to them
at home. This desire is expressed frequently in many of the songs.

There is considerable evidence that a good many emigrants
were in fairly comfortable circumstances when they left the
homeland. Officials, concerned about adverse effects on the
economy, complained about the large sums of capital they were
taking with them.[42] Many others who had little or no resources
soon attained a respectable status abroad; in the words of one
bard:

Daoine bochda, sìol nan coiteir,
Bha gun stochd gun bhuar;
'S mairg a chàin i, tìr an àigh,
'S an dràsd' iad na'n daoine uaisl'.[43]

Poor people, sons of cottars,
without stock or cattle;
it is not fitting to dispraise the land of promise
where they are now respected men.

Generally speaking, Gaels cherished their heritage and endeavoured to perpetuate it wherever their fortunes brought them. Part of that heritage was their national dress, which was not particularly adaptable to pioneer life. Its proscription after the '45 had given it a new symbolism; it was a reminder of the heroism and strong loyalty of which the Highlander was capable when he believed in a 'cause.' Although the evidence is scanty, it is known that the kilt was worn by early emigrants long after they had settled abroad. In the 1840s John Maclean remarked that one of his senior neighbours, John the Miller Sutherland, had worn it every day since he had come to Pictou County, Nova Scotia, in 1821.[44] Later on in the century, Piper John MacGillivray composed a song extolling its fine history and the respect it had commanded on many European battlefields.[45] It was the Piper's way of disapproving of his son's recent refusal to purchase a Highland outfit. It was fitting, too, that emigrant bards like the Piper should salute the kilt if their repertoire was to touch on all facets of Highland life.

The first English reference to Highland emigrant songs was made by Samuel Johnson during his visit to Raasay in 1773, when he heard 'a farewell composed by one of the Islanders that was going, in this epidemical fury of emigration, to seek his fortune in *America*.'[46] By that time the genre was already part of the general corpus of Gaelic songs which enlivened gatherings in the homes of the lairds and the lowly. The fury of emigration attracted the attention of recognized bards like John MacCodrum, John Macrae of Kintail, and the great bard of Coll, John Maclean. Obscure and lesser bards were also moved to song by their own experiences or by those of their friends.[47] They, too, witnessed the depopulation of the homeland, and many of them were obliged to leave it. Their songs, like those of their peers, are a genuine expression of and commentary on the woes, uncertainties, and hopes engendered by emigration.

Most of these compositions are now scattered throughout periodicals, newspapers, and anthologies, some of which are very rare, others literally oceans apart. Many have been recorded in Scotland, in Nova Scotia, and in other parts of Canada. Possibly many more have escaped the attention of collectors through whose foresight much of the literary heritage of the Gael has been recovered and preserved.[48]

The present collection is based on the Scottish Gaelic holdings in the libraries of Harvard University and in the Special Collections of the Angus L. MacDonald Library of St Francis Xavier University, Antigonish, Nova Scotia. Most of the texts have been taken from their earliest printed editions; additional lines or stanzas from other texts have been added where it seemed useful and permissible to do so. With due regard for dialectal peculiarities, spelling and contracted forms have been normalized according to the standard set by Edward Dwelly in his *Illustrated Gaelic-English Dictionary* (6th ed, Glasgow 1967). Dialect forms required to fit the patterns of assonance have been retained.

The songs have been selected and arranged according to the specific geographical areas to which they pertain, and they have been drawn from compositions ranging from the late eighteenth to the end of the nineteenth century. Information about the author, the time and place of composition, and other relevant data have been added where possible. A few selections which could not be so documented have been included because of their relevance to a particular area or phase of emigration not otherwise represented. In so far as possible, repetition has been kept to a minimum.

Two significant omissions may require an explanation. Songs by John MacCodrum, pertaining to emigration to North Carolina ca 1774, are not included here since they have already been edited definitively with notes and translation.[49] Undoubtedly the greatest of all emigrant songs, *A' Choille Ghraumach (The Gloomy Forest)*, composed by John Maclean about 1820, has been omitted too. Because of its immense popularity it has been edited repeatedly.[50] It is still recited – all eighteen verses – by Gaelic speakers in Scotland and abroad, and thus it does not fit easily into a collection of less celebrated compositions.

The translations are for the most part as literal as the requirements of both English and Gaelic permit. Where they are similar or identical to some already in print, it is because there are only a limited number of renderings for certain words, phrases, or complete statements. I have tried to match line-for-line, sometimes at the risk of considerable infelicity. There are, of course, passages which simply do not translate, as any native Gaelic speaker knows. In almost all cases the rhythm, imagery, and restraint of the original suffer in translation. Some selections included here are, in fact, far more colourful both in language and in content than the renderings would suggest. For example, in the last stanza of *O, siud an toabh a ghabhainn* (*That is the road I would take*), the redundant "'s cha dean sinn fuireach' ('and we shall not remain') enhances the intensity of the first line; in translation it is just bland repetition. Numerous other examples will be obvious to those who will be irked by them.[51] Indeed an exercise such as this makes one thing painfully clear: if language be 'the pedigree of a people,' the decline of spoken Gaelic can only result in the dilution of our heritage as we become more and more dependent on translations and farther removed from the humour, imagery, and subtlety of the old tongue.

1 The Carolinas

Donald Matheson
(1719-1782)

Donald Matheson, the most distinguished bard in the earldom of Sutherland, was probably born at Kinbrace in Kildonan, where he spent his early manhood.[1] Later he moved with his family to Badanloch in the upper part of Kildonan. There he became a cattle dealer like his contemporary, Rob Donn, the Reay Country bard. Unlike him, Matheson also became a catechist, after which he was considered the chief intellectual and religious influence of his day in Kildonan.

Matheson was the first recorded literary figure in Sutherland for many centuries.[2] His poetry and songs were mostly religious hymns and elegies with occasional reproving satires.[3] Social and political events – even the Jacobite rising of 1745 – seemed hardly to touch him. But emigration did; in its initial stages he recognized the final disintegration of the old patriarchal order to which Rob Donn was deeply attached.[4] His compatriots were oppressed by landlords, some of whom were usurpers. God had foreseen their plight and had provided a distant land to which they would be led from bondage as Moses had delivered the Israelites from Egyptian slavery. The emigrants and their children would prosper. Their letters would testify to their success. From these reflections Matheson fashioned the song, *Tha mi 'faicinn iongantas* (*I see a wonder*), perhaps the first of all Highland

emigrant songs. Internal evidence indicates that it was composed
some time between 1768 and 1771:

> Seirbhisich na'n uachdarain
> 'us oighreachan na'n clann. (lines 21-2)

> Servants have become landlords
> and young children heirs.

The 'young children' were the heirs to the Reay country and to
the earldom of Sutherland respectively. The fifth Lord Reay died
in Edinburgh in 1768 and was succeeded by a young idiot
brother. Two years earlier Earl William of Sutherland had died at
Bath, leaving only an infant daughter to succeed him. Emigration from Sutherland to North America was greatly accelerated
after the young heiress was formally pronounced Countess in
March 1771.[5]

It has been suggested that *Tha mi 'faicinn iongantas* was directed
to a group of emigrants who left Sutherland to go to South Carolina in the reign of George III.[6] This statement is not (to my
knowledge) corroborated in contemporary records. It is certain
that Scottish Covenanters were in South Carolina for almost a

---

THA MI 'FAICINN IONGANTAS

Tha mi 'faicinn iongantas
Air tighinn anns an àm;
Chan eil againn ach bhi 'g éisdeachd
Na chanas Esan ruinn.
5 Buinidh nithean na follaiseach
Dhuinne 'us do'r cloinn,
Ach na nitheanan tha uaigneach
'S e 'dhiamhaireachds' tha ann.

Ach tha mi 'faicinn faileas
10 De nithean bh' ann bho chéin,

century before Donald Matheson composed this song. It is more
difficult to trace the arrival of later groups. Alexander Hewatt,
pastor of the First Presbyterian Church in Charleston from 1760
to 1766, described the plan sponsored by the Colonial Assembly
to attract foreign Protestant emigrants. Large numbers came
from Ireland, only a few from England and Scotland.[7] If emigrants from Sutherland in the 1770s did go to South Carolina,
they would have found that the fixed and favourable designs of
Providence went beyond what their pious catechist predicted for
them. Allegedly, the early planters in the colony had become so
affluent that they had little to do except hunt and fish and ride
their fine horses.[8]

The poetry of Donald Matheson was first published at Tain in
1816, and a second edition appeared in 1825.[9] A copy of the latter was printed at Pictou, Nova Scotia, in 1832, and is the source
of the text of *Tha mi 'faicinn iongantas*, edited here.[10] A few emen-
dations have been made, but care has been taken to retain forms
which appear to be peculiar to the Gaelic dialect of Sutherland in
the late eighteenth century. The song is interesting for its biblical
overtones. It is also a contemporary commentary on significant
social changes in Sutherland long before the clearances of the
notorious Countess Elizabeth in the early part of the nineteenth
century.

I SEE A WONDER

I see a wonder
happening at this time;
we have but to listen
to what He is telling us.
Obvious matters pertain   5
to us and to our children,
but what is mysterious
is His own secret.

I see a reflection
of what happened long ago,   10

Dar bha pobull Israel
'S an Eiphit ann am péin;
Thug e le làmh làidir iad
A mach bho Pharaoh féin;
15 'S dh'fhosgail e an cuan doibh
Dar luathaich e 'n déidh.

Tha mi 'faicinn deuchainnean
An tràthsa air gach làimh;
Teaghlaichean bha urramach
20 Air leagadh mhàn an ceann.
Seirbhisich 'nan uachdarain
'Us oighreachan 'nan clann.
An talamh làn de dh'éiginn –
A Dhé, co sheasas ann!

25 Tha mi faicinn risdich
An fhìrinn air a ceann;
Dorus a bhi air fhosgladh
'N uair a bha an iomairt teann.
'S nam b'e chlann cumhant
30 A dhùraigeadh dhol ann,
Dh'fhosgladh e na flaitheanais
Mus tigeadh iad gu mall.

'S ged theidheadh iad do Char'lina
No do mhìr tha fo'n ghréin,
35 Cha b'urra dhoibh tachairt
Ach ann an talamh féin.
'S iad oighreachan nan geallaidhnean
'S bithidh an solumas da réir,
'S ged thigeadh iad gu cruaidh-chas
40 Theid fuasgladh orr' 'nam feum.

Tha mi faicinn iongantas
Air tighinn anns an àm,
Ach 's e co-lìonadh na fìrinn e
Bha air innseadh dhuinn ro' làimh;

when the Israelites were
in Egypt in distress.
He brought them with a strong hand
away from Pharaoh, himself,
and divided the sea for them   15
when he pursued them.

I see hardships
now on every side;
families who were respected
with their heads brought low;   20
servants become landlords,
and young children heirs.[11]
The land is full of misery.
O God, who can endure it?

Once more I see   25
the truth borne out,
a door being opened
when the rig becomes too narrow.[12]
If the children of the covenant
would wish to go there,   30
He would open the heavens
lest evil should befall them.

If they should go to Carolina
or to any land under the sun,
they could meet   35
only on their own land.
They are heirs of the promises;
their reward will be as ordained;
and although they should be in distress
relief will come in their need.   40

I see a wonder
happening at this time,
it is the fulfilment of a truth
revealed to us long since.

45 Gu'm bitheadh àite aonarach,
    Daoine air 'n cur ann;
    Aig am bitheadh iad air aitearadh
    Le caiteal agus clann.

    Feudaidh an glan 's an salach
50 Bhi 'n aon uair anns an long;
    An cogull 'us an cruithneachd
    Bhi air an cur 's an aon fhonn;
    'Us fàsaidh iad cuideachd
    Gus am bi am foghair ann,
55 Dar thig tìm na dealaichdean
    Eadar cruithneachd agus moll.

    Ma chanas sibh gur breugach seo
    Leughaibh e bho'n tuil,
    'N uair nach robh air fhàgail
60 Ach an airc gu sìol-cuir.
    Ma leughas sibh gu grunnd e
    'S éiginn dhuibh an sguir,
    Ma's breithnich sibh reusant'
    Gach creutair bha 'n siud.

65 Ach 's e tha cur orm iongantas
    Cionnas bha iad beò;
    An t-uan agus am madradh
    Air an cur anns an aon chrò;
    An nathair 'us an duine
70 Chaidh an tùs leatha 'leòn,
    Gach beathach glan 's neo-ghlan,
    Cionnas fhuair iad lòn?

    Ged bhithinn-se cho gòrach
    'S gu'n deònaichinn 'dhol ann,
75 Mur teidinn air an rathad
    Chan fhada bhithinn ann.
    'S ann tha mo shùil ri baile
    'Us fearainn nach bi gann,

There would be a vacant land,   45
and people would be sent there;
there they would settle
with their cattle and their children.

The clean and the unclean may
be in the vessel at the same time;   50
the cockle and the wheat
may be sown in the same soil;
they will grow together
until fall comes
and it is time to separate   55
the wheat from the chaff.

If you say this is untrue,
read it from the account of the flood,
when there was nothing left
but the Ark as the seed of future life.   60
If you read it carefully,
you must reach the same conclusion,
if you make a reasonable judgment about
each creature there.

But what causes me to wonder   65
is how they lived;
the lamb and the wolf
together in the same close;
the serpent and man
whom he had originally wounded;   70
each animal, clean and unclean –
how did they get sustenance?

Although I should be so foolish
as to wish to go there,
if I couldn't go by road   75
I would not be there for long.[13]
My eye is raised to a home
where land will not be wanting,

Far nach caochail maighstir
80 'S nach imir cliath no crann.

Tha uachdarain 'nan daorsainn
Do dhaoine anns an àm,
'Gam fuadachadh 's 'gan teannachadh
Gu tìr ni maith do'n clann;
85 Ach moladh bhi gu bràch
Do 'n Ti is àirde glòir,
Fhuair a mach am fosgladh ud
'S dheasaich dhoibh an lòn.

'S e mo bharail air na càirdean
90 Tha 'n tràthsa fada uainn,
Gu'n dean Dia an libhrigeadh
Bho chumhachd gaoith 'us cuain.
Ged [nach] 'eil dàn mar dhùrachd
Aig uaisle an taobh tuath,
95 Gheibhear an cuid litrichean
'Us teisteanas am buaidh.

John Macrae / Iain MacMhurchaidh
(? -1780?)

John Macrae, Iain MacMhurchaidh (John, Son of Murdoch), was
a bard of considerable merit and great popularity before he emigrated from Kintail to North Carolina around 1774.[1] He is said
to have been a grand-nephew of Duncan Macrae to whom the
Fernaig manuscript is ascribed. As a youth, he had been ground
officer, deer stalker, and forester on the Earl of Seaforth's estates
in Kintail and Lochalsh. By his own admission he was more
inclined to the chase and the dram than to any serious pursuits.
In one of his songs he characterized himself as 'maor gòrach an
uisge-bheatha' (foolish officer addicted to whisky).[2] In another,
addressed to his wife, he revealed his innate indolence:

where the master will not change,
and neither harrow nor plough will be needed. 80

Landlords are enslaving
their people at this time,
evicting and forcing them
to a land of prosperity for their children.
Praise be eternally 85
to Him of highest glory
who opened a way out there
and prepared a livelihood for them.

My expectation for the kinsfolk,
now far from us, 90
is that God will deliver them
from the power of wind and sea;
and although Providence may not accord with our wishes[14]
for the worthy folk of the Highlands,
their own letters will arrive 95
to testify to their success.

Mi gun chosnadh 'na mo nàdur
O'n là chaidh mo bhaisteadh;
'S mór gu'm b'fheàrr mo chuir 'n a' chìll
No na mhìll mi de thasdain.

'S olc an céile do mhnaoi òig
D'am bu chòir a bhi maiseach,
Fear nach cumadh rithe riamh
Bonn a riaraicheadh ceart i.[3]

I have been by nature disinclined to work
from the day I was baptized.

It would be better that I were in the grave
than that I have squandered so many shillings.

A poor husband for the young lady,
elegant in her own right,
is the man who would never provide
means befitting her.

This last statement gives some support to the tradition that Macrae's wife was Miss MacKenzie of Davochmaluag, whose mother was a daughter of MacKenzie of Fairburn, a well-to-do tacksman.[4] According to other accounts the bard married Christena, daughter of Alexander Roy MacLean of Torloisich.[5] One of his songs alludes to his rejection by Helen, daughter of Donald Macrae, also of Torloisich.[6] As will be seen later in one of his songs, he remembered the Torloisich family with affection after he had gone to America.

In his native Kintail, Iain MacMhurchaidh was extremely popular with farmer, cottar, and laird alike. When he decided to go to America, friends tried to dissuade him. Three of the leading landlords in Ross offered him any farm on their estates. But many of his neighbours were emigrating to North Carolina. Some had already gone, and their reports were impressive. Around 1774 the bard bade farewell to kith and kin on the heights of Auchtertyre in Lochalsh and then boarded an emigrant ship at Cailleach. His wife, a daughter, and three sons, Charles, Murdoch, and Donald, went with him. Another daughter remained in Scotland at Fardoch and married Finlay Macrae.[7]

Traditional accounts of John Macrae's fate in North Carolina give very little detail. He joined the Royalist forces in the Revolutionary War and was taken prisoner at the Battle of Moore's Creek, 27 February 1776. He was treated with great severity by his captors, allegedly because of the inflammatory and patriotic tone of his songs. One tradition has it that he died in a dungeon; according to another, less well known, he was drawn by horses. Although his songs from this period are revelatory, they do not give specific indications as to why and where he was a fugitive.

His only direct reference is to Cornwallis whose coming he hopefully awaits.[8]

Recently the Reverend James MacKenzie has established tentatively that on 27 April 1775 the bard purchased 150 acres of land between Richland and McLendon's Creek in Cumberland (now Moore) County.[9] In the Cumberland County Tax List for 1780 this property was assessed triple the amount ordinarily levied, a common penalty for a Loyalist. Since Macrae was listed as a Loyalist, his whereabouts may have been unknown. A Loyalist claim, dated at Cape Fear, North Carolina, 29 February 1784,[10] indicates that McLendon's Creek was almost deserted by then; only Donald Campbell's family and his daughters, Mrs MacLeod and Mrs Bethune (the mother of the Reverend John Bethune), remained there. In his song *Sgeula a thuair mi bho Dhi-dòmnuich* (*News I received since Sunday*) Macrae says that before he emigrated he received a letter from a John Bethune who had preceded him to North Carolina.[11] From these loose strands of evidence, it would appear that McLendon's Creek was the bard's home for as long as he had a fixed domicile in America.

Most of John Macrae's songs might have been lost were it not for a long-lived informant in Kintail who recited them about 1880 to Alexander MacKenzie, editor of the *Celtic Magazine*, as he had done forty years earlier for John MacKenzie, editor of the well known *Sàr Obair nam Bàrd Gaidhealach*.[12] MacKenzie had incorporated Macrae's songs, together with those of Alastair Grant and Alastair MacIver, in a Prospectus drawn up for a second edition of *Sàr Obair*, but he died in 1848 before the manuscript reached the printers, and subsequently the part of it containing the works of all three bards was lost. Years later Alexander MacKenzie sought out the original informant and recovered practically all of the Macrae songs as well as biographical information about the bard, which he then published in the *Celtic Magazine*.[13]

It is, of course, unwise to attribute the survival of any part of the Gaelic tradition to any one person or milieu. The Kintail bard was well known in Strathglass. Business and pleasure drew him there, and many of his songs were familiar to residents of that area.[14] In a paper read to the Gaelic Society of Inverness, 3 February 1886, Colin Chisholm stated that he knew and could recite several of Macrae's songs when he left his native Strathglass fifty years before. He also referred to a large manuscript collection made available to him by its owner, Captain Alexander Matheson of Dornie; the two Macrae songs included in his paper were taken from that collection.[15]

In 1889 the Reverend Alexander Macrae published his history of the Clan Macrae in which he included texts and translations of three of the bard's songs but did not indicate his sources for these. He may have known them by oral tradition. He may have compared notes with Alexander MacKenzie and with Colin Chisholm; textual variants indicate that he did not draw direct from either. His account of the bard agrees substantially with that of MacKenzie. In any case, we are indebted to these three editors for the first printed versions of John Macrae's songs and for pertinent details about the bard's life.

In the fall of 1775 another John Macrae, Iain Mac a' Ghobha (John the blacksmith's son), bought a plantation of 150 acres in Anson County, North Carolina, and was comfortably settled there before he joined the Royalist forces early in 1776. He served under Captain Alexander MacLeod, marched with the Highlanders at Moore's Creek, and there lost an arm and was taken prisoner. In December 1782 he was in London, still pressing for attention to a claim which had been filed for him at Charleston, South Carolina, on 8 January of that year. Through the intervention of Governor Josiah Martin he was awarded £120 on his property loss and given a yearly pension of £30.[16] Subsequently, Iain Mac a' Ghobha returned to Scotland where he was known as 'fear na leith làimh' (the one-armed man). Possessed of a fine voice and a good memory, he brought back to the old country many of the songs of the bard of Kintail. More than likely it is to him that we owe the preservation of those which were composed in America. 'Fear na leith làimh' died at Candu near Dornie in 1839 at the age of ninety-three.[17]

Iain MacMhurchaidh's songs are among the very earliest of the genre which have come down to us.[18] Almost certainly he was the only one of his time who left a record in song of the emigrant scene on both sides of the Atlantic. The eight songs edited here pertain directly to emigration. In these the bard sings about leaving his homeland; he sings on board the emigrant vessel; and finally he sings of the loneliness of the strange life in America and his misfortune there. Although we know nothing about him after 1776, he has not been forgotten, and recent interest in his life and poetry gives some assurance that he will always hold a place of honour in the annals of Scottish Gaelic bards.

Leaving his homeland was as painful to John Macrae as it was to hundreds of his fellow emigrants. In the first two songs below it is obvious that, before setting out himself, he wished to know something of the fortunes of those who had gone before him. Clearly, conditions at home had become insufferable, especially for those who did not produce to the satisfaction of landlords. In *B'fheàrr leam gu'n cluinnin uaibh sgeula* (*I wish I would get news from you*) the bard alludes to the landless retainers who in former times were so gallant in battle and are now scorned and neglected by their own people. He longs for news of those who survived the voyage to the New World.[19] When news does come, as noted in *Sgeula a fhuair mi bho Dhi-dòmhnuich* (*News I received since Sunday*), it is not highly encouraging.[20] Yet, it is better to go out to the land of plenty than to remain in subjection to avaricious landlords at home.

In the first part of another song, *Bho na sguir mi phàidheadh màil* (*Since I have ceased to pay rent*) the bard appears to be a spokesman for his dispossessed friends.[21] According to tradition he, himself, was in fairly comfortable circumstances. It may be inferred from his reflections in this song that he scorned extreme frugality and meanness. He spent recklessly, but through good fortune his resources were always certain. Evidently he had sold out by the time he composed the song and was hoping that no official or other obstacle would prevent him from emigrating.

John Macrae is said to have invited the captain of the emigrant vessel to dine with him before they sailed for America. The captain was impressed with the fine fare set before him, warned his host that he could not live so well abroad, and tried to discourage his going. But the bard had already made up his mind, and his intentions were known to his friends, many of whom he had urged to emigrate with him. He could not desert them now nor could he risk his honour by doing so at the last minute. Once on board ship he composed the spirited song, *Nise bho na thachair sinn* (*Now that we have met*),[22] to encourage them and to convince them of the need to escape servile conditions at home.

Perhaps the best known of all of John Macrae's songs is the lullaby *Dean cadalan sàmhach, a chuilean mo rùin* (*Sleep softly, my darling beloved*), also known as *Duanag Altrum* (Lullaby).[23] This song is still known in many parts of the Gaelic-speaking world. In 1922 the *Casket* asked its readers whether it was known to them. The response indicated that it was familiar to residents in various areas of eastern Nova Scotia.[24] In 1937, John Lorne Campbell of Canna recorded it in Cape Breton.[25] As might be expected, it is still popular in Kintail. Some years ago the late James C.M. Campbell, a native of Dornie, recorded it during a BBC broadcast devoted to the life and songs of John Macrae.

Dean cadalan sàmhach was probably addressed to the bard's daughter after the family had emigrated to America. The 'darling beloved' is assured of security and abundance in the New World if she but prove herself worthy of one of the many eligible suitors who will present themselves. For the bard, himself, prospects are not so cheery; he dislikes the residents around him, the forbidding forest overawes him, and he can never escape the gnawing nostalgia that calls him back to Kintail.

Leig dhiot an cadal, a chuilean mo rùin (*Be done with sleep, my*

B'FHEARR LEAM GU'N CLUINNINN UAIBH SGUELA

B'fhearr leam gu'n cluinninn uaibh sgeula
Ciamar tha sibh 'n déidh na mara.
  Togamaid fonn air na feara,
  Dh'fhalbh uainn a null 's a chaidh thairis;
5 Togamaid fonn air na feara.

darling beloved), published by Thomas Sinton in the *Poetry of Badenoch*,[26] appears to be a variant of *Dean cadalan sàmhach*. Sinton does not give the author's name, but he does state that the song was composed in America. It is a strange mixture of counsel, self-revelation, and longing for the homeland. Although the form suggests an exchange between the bard and his daughter, it may be a subtle allegory, inspired by reflections on the unhappy consequences of indolence.

Gur muladach a tha mi (*Lonely am I*) is a Loyalist song, composed some time after the outbreak of the American Revolution.[27] Here the bard contrasts the uncertainty and distress of the times with former happy days in Kintail. He reminisces about the homeland and recalls the thrill of stalking stately stags in the deer forest. There is little to cheer him now. The disloyalty of the rebels irks him and strengthens his resolution to stand fast by the king. The song seems to corroborate a tradition, still current in Scotland, that Macrae was betrayed into the hands of the Patriots by fellow Scots.[28] Certainly the song is addressed to Gaels – Gaels who had deserted the royalist cause. The bard warns them, in terms redolent of post-Culloden days, of the terrible consequences of their defection.

In a final song, John Macrae is worn and weary as he sings about his exile and imprisonment in the 'land of misery.' *'S mi air fògradh bho fhoghair* (*I have been a fugitive since autumn*) is the cheerless chant of a fugitive who has done his duty by his king, for by ancient Celtic tradition the king had a right to his service. Perhaps Cornwallis will come soon; if so, the bard will join him eagerly, and his captors will have due retribution.[29]

I WISH I WOULD GET NEWS FROM YOU

I wish I would get news from you
of how you are after the crossing.
    Let us sing about the men
    who have left us and gone across;
    let us sing about the men.   5

'M bi sibh 'g iarraidh tuilleadh chàirdean
Dh'fhios an àite d'rinn sibh fantainn?

Tha sinn an seo troimh a' chéile
Leis gach sgeul' a tha-sa 'g aithris.

10 'S iomadh fear tha ann am breislich,
'N dùil ri teisteanas mun earrach.

'M fear tha falamh chan 'eil diù dha
Ge b'fheàrr e na triùir an carraid.

Aig uachdaran cha bhi spéis dha
15 Bho nach fhaic e 'spréidh 's na gleannaibh.

'M fear 'g am bi nì cuirear sàradh ann
Gus am pàidhear màl an fhearainn.

Cuiridh dhaoine féin e suarach;
'S e mo thruaighe 'n duine falamh.

20 Fhir thairg am baile fo bhàrr dhomh,
Gu'n d'fhàg thu mo bhràthair falamh.

SGEULA A FHUAIR MI BHO DHI-DOMHNUICH

Sgeula a fhuair mi bho Dhi-dòmhnuich
Ar leam nach b'i 'chòir a bh'aca.
  Thogainn fonn, fonn, fonn,
  Dh'éireadh fonn oirnn ri 'fhaicinn.

5 Litir a fhuair mi bho Iain Béitean
Chuir éibhneas air fear nach fhac i.

Beagan a mhuinntir mo dhùthcha
Triall an taobh am faigh iad pailteas.

35 John Macrae / Iain MacMhurchaidh

Would you ask more of your friends
[to come] to the place where you have settled?

Here we are confounded
by the reports being given.

Many are confused,   10
hoping for information by spring.[30]

One who has nothing is ignored
although better he than three men in time of strife.[31]

His chief has no regard for him
because he sees not his herd in the glens.   15

He who has property will be distrained
until his land rent is paid.

His own people will despise him;
pity the man of no means.

You who offered me a flourishing farm[32]   20
have left my brother propertyless.

THE NEWS I RECEIVED SINCE SUNDAY

The news I received since Sunday
appears to me not to be right.
    I would raise a song;
    we would be moved to song on seeing it.

A letter I got from John Bethune   5
gave joy only to him who didn't see it.

A few of my compatriots
are going to a land where they will have plenty.

Falbhamaid 's bitheadh beannachd Dhé leinn;
10   Triallamaid 's riadhamaid barca.

B'fhearr na bhi fuireach fo uachdarain
Nach fhuiling tuath a bhi aca;

A ghabhadh an t-òr an àite 'n t-seòid,
Ged a bhiodh e 'n spòg a'phartain;

15   A ghabhadh an àite an diùnlaoich
An slaodaire lùgach 's e beartach.

Falbhaidh sinn uile gu léir
('S beag mo spéis do dh'fhear gun tapadh),

Far am faigh sinn dheth gach seòrsa
20   An t-sealg is bòidhche tha ri fhaicinn.

Gheibh sinn fiadh 'us boc 'us maoisleach,
'S comas na dh'fhaodar thoirt asda.

Gheibh sinn coileach-dubh 'us liath-chearc,
Lachan, ialtan, 'us glas-gheòidh.

25   Gheibh sinn bradan agus ban-iasg,
Glas-iasg ma 's e 's fheàrr a thaitneas.

Nach saoil thu nach iad siud tha uallach.
Cha bhi buachaille gun each ac'.

BHO NA SGUIR MI PHAIDHEADH MAIL

Bho na sguir mi phàidheadh màil
'S gu'n ruith mo chuid as mo làimh,
'S ann a bhitheas mi 'na mo thràill
Fo nàbuidh bh'agam roimhe seo.

37 John Macrae / Iain MacMhurchaidh

Let us go and may God's blessing be with us.
Let us go and charter a vessel.[33]   10

Better that than to remain under landlords
who will not tolerate tenantry;

who would prefer gold to a brave man,
though it be in the crab's claw;[34]

who would prefer instead of a handsome hero   15
the bandy-legged cheat with his wealth.

We shall all go together –
small is my esteem for the man without heroism –

to where we shall find every kind
of the most beautiful game to be seen.   20

We shall get deer, buck, and doe,
and the right to take as many as we wish.

We shall get woodcock and woodhen,
teals, ducks, and wild geese.

We shall get salmon and spawning fish   25
and white fish if it please us better.

Imagine how prosperous they are over yonder;
even every herdsman has a horse.[35]

SINCE I HAVE CEASED TO PAY RENT

Since I have ceased to pay rent
and my property has gone from my hands,
I shall be a bondman
to my former neighbour.

₅ Ho, chan eil mulad oirnn.
Carson a bhiodh mulad oirnn?
Mulad chan eil oirnn no gruaim;
Gur fada bhuainn a ghabhadh e.

'N uair a dh'éireas esan moch
₁₀ Feumaidh mise 'dhol a mach;
Saoil sibh féin nach cruaidh an t-achd
A bhi fo smachd an atharraich.

Teirgidh 'chuid dha'n duine chrìon
Nach d'rinn bonn do dh'fhialachd riamh;
₁₅ Their fear eile sin nach fhiach
A chaith e trian dheth lathaichean.

Mairidh chuid dha'n duine chòir;
Gheibh càch dheth furan gu leòr.
Bidh pailteas aige ri bheò
₂₀ Ged 's neònach le fear gleidhidh e.

Cridhe farsuing 'us e fial,
Coisnidh 's caithidh e ri mhiann.
'N uair is fhaisg e air dol sìos,
Thig lìonmhorachd 'na lamhan-sa.

₂₅ Cuir an t-searrag sin a nall;
Biodh i làn gu ruig an ceann.
Olainn slàinte na bheil thall
O chionn 's gu'm faighinn naigheachd orr'.

Bho na reic sinn ar cuid nì
₃₀ 'S gu'n d'fhuair sinn orra 'n dìol-phrìs,
'S duilich leam mar tig an t-sìth,
Nach leig an Rìgh an rathad leinn.

Togaidh sinn iorram le fonn
Bho nach buinig a'chaochla' bonn;

We are not lonely   5
Why should we be lonely?
We are neither lonely nor dejected;
far be it from us [to be so].

When he arises early
I must go outside;   10
imagine how irksome it is
to be under a stranger's domination.

The wealth of the miser will dwindle,
for he was never given to generosity;
another will say that what he has spent   15
in a third of his life is not worth the effort.

The gentle man's means will not diminish
though his bounty extends to all.
He will have plenty always
to the astonishment of the frugal one.   20

A kind, open-hearted one
will earn and spend at will;
when he is close to penury
abundance will come into his hands.

Fetch that stoup here;   25
let it be filled to the brim.
Let me drink to those who are yonder
that I may get news of them.

Since we have sold our possessions
and received a fitting price for them,   30
I shall be sad if peace does not follow,
if the King will prevent our going.[36]

We shall lift our oars with song,
since other measures will not gain us a penny.

35 Gheibh sinn na phàidheas an long,
'S na chuireas fonn fo mhnathan dhuinn.

NISE BHO NA THACHAIR SINN

Nise bho na thachair sinn,
Fo's cionn an stòip 's na creachaige,
Gu'n òl sinn air na faicinne
'S na cairtealan 's an téid sinn.
5 Tha tighinn fodham, fodham, fodham,
Tha tighinn fodham, fodham, fodham,
Tha tighinn fodham agus fodham,
Tha tighinn fodham éiridh.

Mhnathan, togaibh an t-urras,
10 Sguiribh dheth na h-iomadan;
Cha bharail leam gu'n tillear mi
Bho'n sguir mi dh'ioman spréidhe.

Mhnathan, sguiribh chùbarsnaidh
Bho'n char sibh fo na siùil a stigh;
15 Cha bharail leam gu'n lùbar sinn
Ri dùthaich bhochd na h-éiginn.

H-uile cùis ga theannachadh,
An t-àrdachdainn 's e ghreannaich sinn;
Lìn-mhora bhi 'g an tarruinn,
20 'S iad a' sailleadh na cuid éisg oirnn.

Gur iomadh latha sàraichte
Bha mi deanamh dìge 's gàrraidhnean;
An crodh a' faighinn bàis oirnn
'S mi pàidheadh màil gu h-éigneach.

25 'S iomadh latha dosgainneach
A bha mi giùlan cosguis dhuibh;

We'll have enough to pay for our passage   35
and to provide comfort for our women.

NOW THAT WE HAVE MET

Now that we have met
over the stoup and drinking shell,
we'll drink to what we envision
in the lands to which we are going.
  I am impelled, impelled, impelled,   5
  I am impelled, impelled, impelled,
  I am impelled, and impelled,
  I am impelled to rise.

Women, brace yourselves for the journey;
be done with lamenting.   10
I don't think I can be dissuaded
since I have ceased to herd cattle.

Women, restrain your anxiety
for you have been sheltered under sails;
I don't think we can be induced [to return]   15
to the land of bitter want.

Everything is being tightened.
The raising of rents has alienated us;
great nets are being hauled,
and they are prospering from our fish.   20

Many a toilsome day
I made dykes and hedges;[37]
our cattle were dying
while I paid rent with great difficulty.[38]

Many an unlucky day   25
I bore expenses on your account.

'N uair reidheadh a' chùis gu osburnaich
Bha mi ag osnaich mu'n déighinn.

Mollachd air an uachdaran
30 A chuir cho fad' air chuaintean sinn,
Airson beagan a mhàl suarach
'S cha robh buannachd aige fhéin dheth.

DEAN CADALAN SAMHACH, A CHUILEAN MO RUIN

Dean cadalan sàmhach, a chuilean mo rùin;
Dean fuireach mar tha thu, 's tu an dràsd' an àit' ùr.
Bidh òigearan againn, làn beairteis 'us cliù,
'S ma bhios tu 'nad airidh, 's leat fear-eiginn dhiubh.

5   Gur ann an America tha sinn an dràsd',
Fo dhubhar na coille, nach teirig gu bràth.
'N uair dh'fhalbhas an dùlachd 's a thionndaidh's am
blàths,
Bithidh cnothan, bidh ùbhlan 's bithidh an siùcar a'fàs.

'S ro bheag orm féin na daoine seo th'ann,
10 Le 'n còtaichean drògaid, ad mhór air an ceann;
Le 'm briogaisean goirid, 's iad sgaoilte gu 'm bonn;
Chan fhaicear an t-osan, 's i' bhochdainn a th'ann.

Tha sinne 'n ar n-Innseanaich, cinnteach gu leòir;
Fo dhubhar nan craobh, cha bhi h-aon againn beò;
15 Madaidh alluidh 'us béistean ag éigheach 's gach fròig;
Gu bheil sinne 'nar n-éiginn bho'n là thréig sinn Rìgh
Deòrs'.

Thoir mo shoraidh le fàilte Chinn t-Sàile nam bó,
Far 'n d'fhuair mi greis m' àrach 's mi'm phàisde beag òg.
Bhiodh fleasgaichean donn air bonnaibh ri ceòl,
20 Agus nìonagan dualach 's an gruaidh mar an ròs.

43 John Macrae / Iain MacMhurchaidh

When matters came to ruin,
I sighed over them.

A curse upon the landlord
who sent us far to sea   30
for the sake of a paltry rent
which was of little profit to himself.

SLEEP SOFTLY, MY DARLING BELOVED

Sleep softly, my darling beloved.
Stay as you are, now that you are in a new land.
We'll find suitors abounding in wealth and fame,
and, if you are worthy, you shall have one of them.

We are now in America,   5
in the shade of the never-ending forest.
When winter departs and warmth returns,
nuts, apples, and sugar will grow.

Little do I like the people who are here,[39]
with their drugget coats, tall hats on their heads,   10
and their short breeches split to the ends.
Hose are never seen, and that is a pity.

We've become Indians surely enough.
Skulking under trees, not one of us will be left alive,
with wolves and beasts howling in every lair.   15
We've come to ruin since the day we forsook King George.

Bear my farewell and greeting to Kintail and its cattle,
where I spent my time of upbringing when I was a young child.
There dark-haired lads would dance heel and toe to the music,
and lassies with flowing tresses and cheeks like the rose.   20

An toiseach an fhoghair bu chridheil ar sunnd,
Am fiadh anns an fhireach, 's am bradan an grunnd;
Bhiodh luingeas an sgadain a' tighinn fo shiùil;
Bu bhòidheach a' sealladh 's fir dhonn air am bùird.

LEIG DHIOT AN CADAL, A CHUILEAN MO RUIN

Leig dhiot an cadal, a chuilean mo rùin
Dean moch-éirigh maidne 's gur fheàirrde do chliù;
'Us gheibh thu fear fearainn 'us òigear ùr,
'S gu'm b'fheàrr dhuit siud agad na cadal an cùil.
5   O, 's e an cadal a mheall mi riamh,
Aig truimead mo chridhe 's e tighinn cho dian,
'S ged gheibhinns' fear-fearainn a mharbhadh am fiadh,
Gu'm b'fheàrr leam an cadal no na chunna' mi riamh.

Leig dhiot an cadal 's tu 'd phàisdean òg;
10   Faiceam do bhreacan, do phlaid, 'us do chlò
Air féill 'us air faighir, ri aighear 's ri ceòl,
'S gu'm b'fheàrr dhuit siud agad na cadal am fròig.

Ged gheibhinns' an t-òigear is bòidhch' tha 's an tìr,
Is grinne a sheasas an clachan no 'n cill,
15   Aig ro-mheud a chuideim cha taoghal mo chion;
Cha d'thugainn mo chadalan seachad do 'chionn.

Ach 's ann an America tha sinn an dràsd',
An iomall no coille nach teirig gu bràth;
'N uair dh'fhalbhas an dùlachd 's a thionndas am blàths
20   Bidh cnothan 'us ubhlan gu h-ùrail a' fàs.

Ach 's truagh nach mise bha 'n Geusdo nam bó,
Far an d'fhuair mi m'àrach 'nam phàisdean òg;
Far a' faicte na buachaillean 'cuallach mu'n chrò,
Na nìonagan guanach, 's an gruaidhean mar ròs.

45 John Macrae / Iain MacMhurchaidh

At the onset of harvest-time our spirits would be joyous;
deer on the moors and salmon in the pools;
the herring fleet would come in under sail;
a fine sight with brown-haired lads on board.[40]

BE DONE WITH SLEEP, MY DARLING BELOVED

Be done with sleep, my darling beloved;
rise early in the morning; greater will be your renown,
and you will get a land-owner and a prosperous youth,
and better that than to sleep in hovels.
   Sleep has been my ruin;   5
   I am heavy-hearted, and it envelops me.
   Although I'd get a land-owner who would kill the deer,
   I prefer sleep to all that I have ever seen.

Be done with sleep while you are a young child;
Let me see your tartan, your plaid, and your tweed   10
at festival and market, making mirth and music.
Better that for you than to sleep in a cave.

Although I would get the most beautiful lad in the land,
most noble in status in village or church,
his merit would not sway me;   15
I would not forgo my sleep for it.

We are now in America
at the frontiers of the never ending forest;
when winter goes and warmth returns
nuts and apples will flourish anew.   20

Alas, that I am not in Gesto,[41] land of the cows,
where I was reared as a young child;
where herdsmen could be seen gathering about the fold,
and handsome lassies with cheeks like the rose.

GUR MULADACH A THA MI

Gur muladach a tha mi,
'S mi 'n diugh gun aobhar gàire;
Cha b'ionnan 's mar a bha mi
'S an àite bho thall;
5 Far am faighinn mànran,
Mire, 'us ceòl-gaire,
Agus cuideachd mar a b'àill leam
Aig àilleas mo dhram.
'N uair 'shuidheamaid mu bhòrd ann,
10 Bhiodh botul agus stòp ann;
'S cha b'eagal dhuinn le comh-strì
Ged dh'òlt' na bhiodh ann.
'S e th'againn anns an àite seo
Tarruing dhòrn 'us làmh,
15 Agus cleas nan con bhi sàs
Anns gach àite le'n ceann.

Guidheamaid le dùrachd,
A h-uile fear 'na ùrnaigh,
Gu'n tigeadh lagh na dùthcha
20 Gu cùnntais gun mhall;
Gu'n tigeadh achd bho'n rìgh sin
A b'fhurasd' dhuinn a dhìreadh,
'S a chleachd bhi aig ar sìnnsear
'S an tìm a bha ann.
25 Cha b'e 'm paipear brònach
A shracadh 'na mo phòcaid
Bhiodh againn air son stòrais,
Ach òr gun bhi meallt;
Crodh 'us eich 'us feudail,
30 'G an cunntadh air an réidhlean,
Dheth 'm faighte sealladh éibhinn
Thar eudann nam beann.

LONELY AM I

Lonely am I
today without cause for laughter.
It was not so
in the land beyond [the sea],
where I would get love songs,   5
sport, and cheery music,
and friends to my liking
when I enjoyed my drink.
As we sat around the table,
bottle and stoup were there;   10
we feared no dissension
although we would drink all that was there.
What we have here
is the constant sparring of fists and hands
in the manner of dogs,   15
everywhere with their heads in a fray.[42]

Let us implore,
each one in his prayer,
that the law of the land
may be restored without delay;   20
that a decree will come from the king,
which will be easy for us to observe,
like that known to our forefathers
in days gone by.
It was not wretched paper money,   25
which would tear in one's pocket,
that we used to have as currency,
but genuine gold;
cattle and horses and flocks,
reckoning their numbers on the green;   30
beautiful to behold
on the slopes of the ben.

Mo shoraidh gu Sguir-ùrain
'S an coire th'air a cùlaibh;
35 Gur tric a bha mi dlùth ann
Air chùl agh 'us mhang;
Ag amharc air mo ghlùinean
An damh a' dol 's a' bhùirich
'S a chéil' aige 'ga dùsgadh
40 Air ùrlar nan allt.
Cha b'e 'n duilleag chrianach
A chleachd e bhi 'ga bhiadhadh,
Ach biolar agus mìn-lach
'Us sliabh gun bhi gann;
45 'N uair rachadh e 'ga iarraidh
Gu'n tàirneadh e troimh fhiaclan
An t-uisge cho glan sìolait'
Ri fìon as an Fhraing.

Mo shoraidh leis an fhiadhach,
50 Ged 's tric a bha mo mhiann ann;
Cha mhò ni mi iasgach
Air ìochdar nan allt.
Ged b'ait leam 'ga iarraidh
Le dubhan 'us le driamlach,
55 'S am fear bu ghile bian dhiubh
'Ga shiabadh mu'm cheann.
'Ga tharruing dha na bruaiche,
Bhiodh cuibhle 'dol mu'n cuairt leis,
'Us cromag ann 'ga bhualadh
60 Mu'n tuaims a bhiodh ann.
Ach 's e th'againn anns an àite seo
Cruipin-hoe 's làmhag,
'S cha'n fhasa leam a' mharlin
Cur tàirnich 'nam cheann.

65 Nam faighte làmh-an-uachdar
Air luchd nan còta ruadha,
Gu'n deanainn seasadh cruaidh
Ged tha 'n uair s' orm teann.

My blessing to Sguir-ùrain[43]
and to the corrie on its far side;
often was I deep within it,   35
behind does and fawns,
on my knees peering
at the stag bellowing
and waking his mate
at the bottom of the burns.   40
Not on decayed leaves
did he feed,
but on water-cresses and chamomile
and abundant mountain grass.
When he went in search of it   45
he would draw through his teeth
the pure, filtered water,
clear as French wine.

Farewell to the deer forest,
often did I enjoy it;   50
I shall not fish again
in the lower streams.
A delight it was to me to angle there
with hook and line;
the finest of the catch   55
I would twirl around my head,
hauling it from the river bank
and the reel running with it,
and the gaff striking
against the weir there.   60
But what we have here
is the cruipin-hoe and hand-axe,
and I find the marlin no easier,[44]
thundering around my head.

If mastery were to be gained   65
over the redcoats,
I would take a firm stand
although my hour may be near.

Ged tha iad 'g 'nar ruagadh,
70 Mar bhric a' dol 's na bruachan,
Gu faigh sinn fhathast fuasgladh
Bho'n uamhas a th'ann.
Ma chreideas sibhs' an fhìrınn
Cho ceart 's tha mi 'g innse,
75 Cho cinnteach ris an dìsne
Gur sibhse bhios an call.
Gur e 'ur deireadh dìbreadh
Air fhad's dha'n cum sibh strì ris;
Na's miosa na mar dh'inntrig,
80 'S gur cinnteach gur h-ann.

Siud a' rud a dh'éireas
Mar dean sibh uile géilleadh,
'N uair thig a chuid as tréine
Dhe'n treud a tha thall;
85 Bithidh crochadh agus reubadh,
'Us creach air ar cuid spréidhe;
Chan fhaighear lagh no reusan
Do reubaltaich ann.
Air fhad 's dha'n gabh sibh fògar
90 Bi ceartas aig Righ Deòrsa;
Cha bharail dhomh gur spòrs dhuibh
An seòl 'chaith sibh ann.
Ach 's culaidh ghrath 'us dhéisinn
Sibh fhad 's dha'n cum sibh streup ris;
95 'S gur h-aithreach leibh 'na dhéigh seo
An leum 'thug sibh ann.

'S MI AIR FÒGRADH BHO FHOGHAIR

'S mi air fògradh bho fhoghair,
'Deanamh thaighean gun cheò unnta;
Tha mi sgìth dhe'n fhògar seo,

Even though they are routing us
like trout hiding under river banks,   70
we shall get relief yet
from this awesome plight.
If you believe the truth,
as sure as I say it,
as sure as dice,   75
it is you who will lose.
Your destiny is to fail
as long as you contest him;[45]
a worse state than the first
is sure to follow.   80

This is what will happen
if you do not all yield;
when the strongest forces
from the other side will arrive
there will be hanging and destruction,   85
and raiding of your cattle.
Neither law nor reason will prevail
to protect rebels.
As long as you are in revolt
King George will have the right on his side.   90
I do not think it trifling
the way you have gone.
Rather, you are an object of terror and contempt
as long as you continue to fight him;
later on you will regret   95
the leap you have taken.

I HAVE BEEN A FUGITIVE SINCE AUTUMN

I have been a fugitive since autumn,
building huts with no smoke rising from them.
    I am weary of this exile;

Tha mi sgìth dhe'n t-strì;
5   Seo an tìr dhòruinneach.

Ann am bothan beag barraich,
'S nach tig caraid dha m'fheòraich ann.

Ged a tha mi fo'n choille,
cha'n 'eil coire ri chòmhdach orm;

10   Ach bhi cogadh gu dìleas,
Leis a' rìgh bho'n bha chòir aige.

Thoir mo shoraidh le dùrachd
Gu'n dùthaich 's am bu chòir dhomh bhi.

Thoir mo shoraidh Chinn t-Saìile
15   Far am bi mànran 'us òranan;

A'n tric a bha mi mu'n bhuideal
Mar ri cuideachda shòlasaich.

Cha b'e 'n dram bha mi 'g iarraidh,
Ach na b'fhiach an cuid stòraidhean.

20   Ceud soraidh le dùrachd
Gu Sguir-ùrain, 's math m' eòlas innt'.

'S tric a bha mi mu'n cuairt dhi
Ag éisdeachd udlaich a' crònanaich.

A'bheinn ghorm tha mu coinneamh
25   Leam bu shoillear an neòinean innt'.

Sios 'us suas troimh Ghleann-Seile,
'S tric a leag mi 'n damh cròcach ann.

Gheibhte breac air an linne,
Fir 'gan sireadh 'us leòis aca.

53 John Macrae / Iain MacMhurchaidh

I am weary of strife;
this is the land of misery.   5

In a small brushwood hut
where no friends will come to inquire about me.

Although I am a fugitive
no charge can be laid on me

except loyal service to my king   10
to which he is entitled.

Bear my sincere greeting to the land
where I ought to be.

Bear my greeting to Kintail
where there is music and song.   15

Often was I by the keg
with pleasant company about me.

It was not the dram I sought
but their excellent stories.

A hundred fond greetings   20
to Sguir-ùrain, well do I know it.

Often did I scout around it
listening to the stag bellowing,

and the blue mountain opposite it –
brilliant to me were its flowers.   25

Up and down throughout Glen Shiel[46]
I frequently felled the antlered stag.

Trout were to be gotten in the loch;
lads sought them with a torch.

30 Tha mi nis air mo dhìteadh
Ann am prìosan droch-bheò-shlainteach.

Ach nan tigeadh Cornwallis
'S mi gu falbhadh leis sòlasach

Gu sgrios a thoir air béistean
35 Thug an t-éideadh 's an stòras bhuam.

I am now condemned   30
to an uninhabitable prison.

If Cornwallis would come
I'd go with him gladly

to wreak destruction on the wretches
who took my clothing and property.   35

2 Nova Scotia

Michael MacDonald / Micheil Mór MacDhòmhnaill
(ca 1745-1815)

Michael MacDonald, captain and poet, was born on South Uist around 1745.[1] In 1772 he emigrated to Prince Edward Island with the Glenaladale pioneers,[2] along with Robert Innes, mason of Blair Atholl, and Allan MacDonnell of Glengarry. There is some evidence that at least one of MacDonald's brothers came out, too, either with this group or shortly afterwards. Hugh MacEachern of Kinlochmoidart and his family were fellow emigrants;[3] MacDonald later married Ann MacEachern, and Innes and MacDonnell married her sisters. The future Bishop Angus of Charlottetown was Ann MacEachern's brother.[4]

Micheil Mór spent much of his pioneer life in Judique, Cape Breton. It is commonly held that he was there alone during the winter of 1775. His experiences as the only 'white man' among the Indians were recounted in dramatic detail by a nineteenth-century antiquarian.[5] Some time later he returned to the Island but only temporarily. In 1797 he was back in Judique with Innes and MacDonnell. The MacEachern family were in fairly comfortable circumstances and did not settle on Glenaladale's estate in Prince Edward Island. Perhaps a desire for similar independence motivated Michael and his brothers-in-law to seek grants of land at Judique on the western shore of Cape Breton Island, rather than accept the long-term leases offered by Glenaladale.[6]

The property which the bard and his family occupied can be identified with certainty today.[7] It is not so easy to date the period of occupancy. Within a few years Michael sold out and returned to Prince Edward Island once more. He then settled near the Hillsborough River.[8]

Adventure at sea as well as on land was very much a part of the bard's life. It is related that on one occasion (ca 1812) when returning from Quebec he was attacked by a Yankee privateer. He was forced to surrender, and the Yankees boarded his ship. There were two boxes on board addressed to his brother-in-law, Father Angus which the Yankees respected when they learned that it contained vestments and other altar accessories. They transferred the sacred loot together with the captain and his crew to their own ship, set the captured vessel on fire, and before long landed the captives and boxes safely home again.[9] Whether or not Michael returned to sea after this incident is unknown. He spent the last winter of his life with the Retland MacDonalds in Judique, with whom he had close family connections. He died the following year, 1815, at his home in Prince Edward Island.[10]

O, 'S ALAINN AN T-AITE

O, 's àlainn an t-àite
Th' agam 'n cois na tràghad
'N uair thig e gu bhith 'g àiteach ann
Leis a' chrann, leis a' chrann, O.
5   Ni mi 'n t-aran leis na gearrain
'S an crodh-bainne chuir mu'n bhaile;
'S cha bhi annas oirnn 's an earrach,
Chuirinn geall, chuirinn geall.

O, 's fraoidhneasach, daoimeanach,
10   Glan mar sholus choinnlean,
Am bradan le chuid shoillseanach
Anns gach allt, anns gach allt, O.
Mear ri mire, leum na linne,

It was during the winter of 1775 that Mìcheil Mór is said to have composed the only one of his songs now extant, *O, 's àlainn an t-àite* (*Fair is the place*). According to tradition he was a very fine bard. At least four of his songs were known in Cape Breton in 1892, but these were never published. By 1895 the Reverend Alexander Maclean Sinclair thought most of Michael's songs were already irrecoverable; yet, in 1937, *O, 's àlainn an t-àite* was recorded in eastern Nova Scotia by John Lorne Campbell of Canna.[11]

Had this single song not been preserved, it is doubtful if Mìcheil Mór's fame as a bard would be known today. The song is of great interest, since it is reasonably certain that it is the oldest extant Gaelic commentary on pioneer life in Cape Breton. If it was composed as early as 1775, the bard must have been contemplating future possibilities rather than the harsh realities of his environment at that time. On that fair site, he observed, the land would be productive, trees would yield fruit and sugar, and on festive occasions there would be mirth and merriment, with pipes resounding over the bay and the mighty forest.[12]

FAIR IS THE PLACE

Fair is the place
I have here by the sea,
when it comes time to till it
with the plough.
I shall make bread-land with horses[13]   5
and put the cows to graze;
we shall not be in want in spring,
I wager.

Sparkling, diamond-like,
clear as candle-light,   10
is the salmon with his brilliance,
in every stream.
Merrily sporting, leaping from the pool,

'S bòidheach, milis leam do ghile;
15 'S iomadh gille bhitheas 'gad shireadh
Anns an àm, anns an àm.

O, 's cùbhraidh na smùidean
A bhitheas dhe na taighean siùcair,
Craobhan troma dlùth dhaibh
20 'S iad gun mheang, 's iad gun mheang, O.
'N àm an fhoghair b'e mo roghainn
A bhi tadhal gus an taghadh;
'S gu'm b'e 'm baothair nach tug oidheirp
Air bhi ann, air bhi ann.

25 Fidhleireachd 's pìobaireachd
Aig gillean La Fhéill Mhìcheil,
A chluinnteadh seach mìle
Nach gann, nach gann, O.
Fir 'us fleasgaich 's iad ri beadradh
30 ...
'S bòidheach, speisealta na beicean
A ni chlann, a ni chlann.

Fear a' Mhuinntir Mheinne / a native of Main or a Menzies (ca 1801)

A song composed by this unknown bard is included here chiefly because its source is of considerable interest. Fear a' mhuinntir Mheinne may have been a native of Main in the parish of Kiltarlity, or it could be that his name was Menzies. In any case, he witnessed the early clearances in Strathglass, and he tried to comfort the unhappy victims.

With the death of Alasdair Og (young Alasdair) Chisholm in 1793, Strathglass entered upon an era of depopulation from which it has never recovered. The heir, Alasdair's brother William, married Elizabeth, daughter of Glengarry, in 1795.[1] It was

delightful and sweet to me is your whiteness;
many a lad will seek you   15
in season.

Fragrant is the aroma
which comes from the sugar houses,
tall, limbless trees
surrounding them.   20
In the fall it is my delight
to stop by to select them for tapping.
He was indeed a fool who did not venture
to come here.[14]

Fiddling and piping   25
by lads on Michaelmas day[15]
can be heard beyond miles
unlimited.
Men and youths conversing;
...   30
neat and reverent the gestures
made by kindred spirits.

---

an ominous alliance for the tenantry, for both the chief and his
lady were eager to exploit the new lucrative business of sheep
farming and neither tenantry nor black cattle could stand in
their way.[2] Consequently scores of Strathglass residents were
numbered among those who sailed on several of the earliest-
known vessels bearing emigrants to Nova Scotia and other parts
of Canada at the turn of the century.[3]

Alasdair Og's daughter Mary remembered the song, *Theid sinn
a dh'America* (*We shall go to America*), which Fear a' mhuinntir
Mheinne had composed for the heavy-hearted emigrants as they

left for the New World. It was from her that Colin Chisholm obtained the four verses of it which he sang to members of the Gaelic Society of Inverness on 14 March 1883.[4] Evidently this lady was more kindly disposed towards her father's tenantry

---

THEID SINN A DH'AMERICA

Théid sinn a dh'America
'S gur h-e ar deireadh falbh ann;
Ni sinn fearainn de'n choille
Far nach teirig airgiod.

5 Gheibh sinn càirdean romhainn ann,
Oifigich ro-ainmeil;
Tha cuid aig a'bheil stòras dhiubh
'S cha b'fhiach iad gròt 'n uair dh'fhalbh iad.

Meòirean chraobh air lùbadh ann
10 Le ùbhlan glas 's dearga;
Gheibh sinn beòir gun chunntas ann
A chuireadh sùrd 's an anfhann.

Marbhphaisg air na tighearnan,
An ruith th' ac' air an airgiod;
15 'S fheàrr leò baidein chaorach
No 'n cuid dhaoine 's iad fo àrmachd.

Donald Chisholm / Dòmhnall Gobha
(1735-1810)

Donald Chisholm, commonly known as Dòmhnall Gobha (Donald the Blacksmith), was a good poet and much respected in his native Strathglass before he emigrated to Nova Scotia in 1803.[1] For over twenty years he had been mountain ranger at

than her greedy uncle; otherwise she would hardly wish to perpetuate a song in which the last quatrain calls down a malediction on covetous landlords, concerned only with sheep and money-making.

WE SHALL GO TO AMERICA

We shall go to America
it is our destiny to go there;
we shall convert the forest to holdings
where money will not run out.

We'll find friends there before us,   5
now renowned professional men;
some of them are wealthy though
they hadn't a groat when they emigrated.

There the branches are laden
with green and red apples;   10
we shall have plenty of ale there
to enliven the dispirited.

A plague on the landlords,
with their greed for money;
they prefer flocks of sheep   15
to their own armed hosts.

A'Chìoch (the Pap) in upper Glen Affric. In addition to his farm at Knockfinn, he rented a part of this mountain, which, to his great regret and for reasons unstated, he lost to the Frasers after many years. It was as if his nursemaid had abandoned him:

Chuir mo bhanaltrum cùl rium;
Chaill mi 'n cupan bha fallain.

Fhuair na Frisealaich còir ort,
'S chaidh mis' fhògar le m'aindeòin.[2]

My nursemaid rejected me;
I lost the nourishing cup.

The Frasers obtained a right to you [the mountain]
and I was cast out against my will.

A more painful separation was yet to come. As already noted, Strathglass tenants were in a precarious situation at the turn of the nineteenth century. Donald the Blacksmith was then an old man. He could no longer turn his hand to any occupation as he had done when he was young and strong. But he saw the ruin of his compatriots at the mercy of their unscrupulous chief, and he recognized that the only alternative was emigration. In his youth he had never contemplated leaving

---

BHA MI ÒG ANN A' STRATHGHLAIS

Bha mi òg ann a' Strathghlais,
'S bha mi 'n dùil nach rachainn as,
Ach bho'n chaidh na suinn fo lic
Nis gabhaidh mi 'n ratreuta.
5   Tha mo cheann-sa niste liath,
'N déidh na chunnacas leam riamh;
'S ged is éiginn dhomh bhith triall,
A shiorrachd, 's beag mo spéis dha.

Ged a tha mo choiseachd trom,
10   Togaidh mi m'aigneadh le fonn;
'S 'n uair a theid mi air an long,
Có chuireas rium geall-réise?

Strathglass; now his friends and his son, who had recently
returned from America, urged him to do so. In his song, *Bha mi
òg ann an Strathghlais* (*I was young in Strathglass*), Donald sets
down in detail his reflections on the eve of his departure.[3]

His friends were happy to have him on board the emigrant
vessel to enliven the dreary ocean voyage with songs and merriment. Evidently their expectations were fulfilled; the bard composed at least one song at sea. Although it is most likely that he
and his fellow emigrants sailed on the *Aurora*, the song is
addressed to the *Flòri*.[4]

According to a local tradition in eastern Nova Scotia, the bard
settled on a farm at Lower South River, Antigonish County.[5] His
son John was one of the first citizens of nearby Heatherton;
presumably he emigrated with his father. Another son was a
member of the Jesuit order and was already in the United States
at the time. Two other sons settled in Cape Breton.[6] Little is now
known about Donald the Blacksmith's life in the New World.
Additional information and some of his songs may yet be brought
to light if some of the family records have been preserved.[7]

I WAS YOUNG IN STRATHGLASS

[When] I was young in Strathglass
I had no thought of leaving there;
now that the gallant men have gone
I, too, shall leave.[8]
    My hair is now grey   5
    after all I have seen;
    although I must set forth,
    I have little zest for doing so.

Though my step is heavy
I will stir my spirit with song.   10
When I embark on the ship,
who will challenge me?

'N tacharan seo th'air ar ceann
Sgiot e dhaoine 's tha iad gann;
15 'S fheàrr leis caoraich chuir am fang
No fir an camp fo fhéileadh.

Comunn càirdeil chan 'eil ann,
Chan 'eil éisdeachd aig fear fann;
Mur cuir thu caoraich ri gleann
20 Bidh tu air cheann na déirce.

'N uair a bha mi làidir, òg,
Dheanainn cosnadh air gach dòigh;
Ach an nis bho'n dh'fhalbh mo threòir,
Tha mi air stòras feumach.

20 Gheibh sinn acraichean bho'n rìgh,
Tighearnan gu'n dean e dhinn;
Cha b'ionnan 's a bhith mar bha 'n linn
Bha pàidheadh cìs do Cheusar.

Na biodh eagal oirbh mu'n chuan;
30 Faicibh mar sgoilt a' Mhuir Ruadh.
Tha cumhachdan an Tì tha shuas
An diugh cho buan 's an ceud là.

'N UAIR THEID FLÒRI 'NA H-ÉIDEADH

'N uair theid Flòri 'na h-éideadh
Cha bu mharcaiche steud-eich
Bhuinigeadh oirre geall-réise
'N uair theid bréid fos a cionn.
5 Faill ill ho ro,
Hill uill ho ro,
Faill ill ho ro,
Ho gu, oh ho, ro hi.

67 Donald Chisholm / Dòmhnall Gobha

The coward who now rules us
evicted his own, few remain;
he prefers sheep in the hills   15
to a kilted retinue.

There is no cordial agreement,
no hearing for the poor man;
if one does not raise sheep in the glens
he brings himself to penury.   20

When I was young and strong
I could earn my living in many ways;
now that my vigour is spent
I am in want.

We shall get grants from the king;   25
he will make us proprietors.
We shall not be like the generations
who paid tribute to Caesar.

Do not fear the sea;
mind how the Red Sea was divided.   30
The powers of God above
are as strong today as on the very first day.

WHEN THE *FLORI* IS RIGGED

When the *Flori* is rigged
not even a rider of swift horses
could challenge her
with her sails unfurled.
    Faill ill ho ro,   5
    Hill uill ho ro,
    Faill ill ho ro,
    Ho gu, oh ho, ro hi.

Tha i barantach, làidir,
10 Tha i caol as a h-earraich;
'S i gu'n sgoilteadh muir gàbhaidh
'N uair a b'àirde na tuinn.

Tha a cairt-iùil an deagh òrdugh
'S tha na sgiobearan eòlach;
15 'S mise dannsa le sòlas
Air a bòrd le ceòl binn.

'S mi nach deanadh dà phàirtidh
Dhe na dh'fhalbh as an àite,
Eadar Barraidh 's Aigeis,
20 Dià mar gheàrd air a linn.

Thughaibh cuimhn' air bhur creideamh
Agus seasaibh ri 'r n-eaglais,
Ged a theireadh fear eile
Gur neo-fhreagarrach i.

25 'S ann do thoiseach nam fortan
Bhi fo dhubhar na croise;
Am fear a dhìobras a coltas
Chì e dhocair ri tìm.

John Maclean / Bàrd Thighearna Chola
(1787-1848)

John Maclean, undoubtedly one of the greatest Gaelic bards who
ever left Scotland, was born at Caolas on Tiree, Argyllshire, on 8
January 1787.[1] Throughout his long life he was a poet at heart
and ill-fitted by temperament for any kind of ordinary occupation. As a youth he tried his hand at shoemaking but soon lost
interest in it. A brief period in the army was no more satisfying,
nor was his experiment in merchandizing. But all the while he

She is confident, strong;
her keel is narrow.   10
She forges through the perilous sea
even when the waves are highest.

Her compass is in good order,
her sailors experienced;
I dance with delight   15
to sweet music on board.

I would not make two parties[9]
of those who left here
between Barra and Aigas;[10]
may God protect his flock.   20

Remember your faith
and stand by your church,
though another would say
it is irrelevant.

It is a mark of favour   25
to be under the shadow of the Cross;
he who would forsake its image
will ultimately see his own ruin.

---

cultivated his rare poetic gift. He was still close to the classic
bardic tradition. He listened to the older people in Tiree, and
from them he acquired a vast knowledge of the genealogy,
poetry, and history of the Highlands. Against the wishes of his
friends and his chief, Alexander MacLean, the laird of Coll, he
and his family sailed from Tobermory to Pictou, Nova Scotia, in
1819. He had an entirely false concept of life in the New World,

seeing himself as a laird on his new estate with his children settled comfortably around him. It was indeed a rude awakening when he found himself face to face with the endless gloomy forest from which he must carve out a livelihood.

His first years at Barney's River, Pictou County, were hard and lean. He was unaccustomed to the kind of labour required of pioneer settlers at that time. His wife, the former Isabella Black, adapted to the rigours of the New World with grace and courage. Later, the bard and Charles, the second oldest of his six children, made a clearing in Glenbard, Antigonish County, where he built a house into which the family moved in January 1831. By then all the children were able to work. The bard continued to compose poetry and songs. There is evidence that he shared his intellectual interests with a number of his neighbours, reading with them some of the Gaelic works from his valuable personal collection.[2] At the end of January 1848, while visiting friends at nearby Addington Forks, he suffered a seizure and died instantly of apoplexy. He was buried in Glenbard cemetery, where today hundreds of tourists as well as local residents stop by to pay tribute to one of the most celebrated of all Highland emigrants.

Bard Maclean published his first volume of poetry in 1818, the year before he emigrated. He composed the famous song, *A'*

AM MEALLADH

Latha grianch, ciatach, àghmhor,
Chaidh mi mach a ghabhail sràide,
Dh'fhaotainn sealladh air an àite –
Tìr nan craobhan àrd 's nan gleannan.
5   O, gur mise th' air mo mhealladh,
    'S cian bho'n dh'fhàg mi gràdh gach caraid;
   O, gur mise th' air mo mhealladh.

Cha b'fhada chaidh mi air m' eòlas
'N uair a thachair duine còir rium,

Choille Ghruamach (*The Gloomy Forest*), soon after he arrived in Pictou County and sent it to Scotland. His friends on Tiree were alarmed at his distress and disenchantment with the New World. They offered to pay his way back and give him a piece of land rent free if he would return, but, once he had survived the initial shock of the wilderness and isolation, he was content to remain in Nova Scotia. According to one tradition, still current, he regretted the devastating description of *A' Choille Ghruamach* and tried to atone for its discouraging effects on emigration in a cheery song, *Am Bàl Gàidhealach* (*The Gaelic Ball*), composed in 1826, when he was invited to a Highland ball at Merigomish.[3]

Only two of Bard Maclean's songs are included here. His works have already received considerable attention, and the songs he composed as an emigrant are too numerous to be included *in toto*. One of those selected, *Am Mealladh* (*The Deception*), is a clever blend of humour and chagrin.[4] It touches on many of the sentiments expressed by the bard in other compositions. *Oran do'n Chuairtear* (*Song for the 'Tourist'*) is a kind of apostrophe to a Gaelic periodical published in Scotland, illustrating the eagerness with which emigrants tried to keep in touch with the old country. Using 'Tourist' metaphorically, the bard indulges in extravagant praise of the Gael, his exploits, and his language.[5]

THE DECEPTION

On a sunny, mild, pleasant day,
I went for a walk
to take a look at the place,
this land of tall trees and valleys.
    Alas, I was deceived;   5
    it is unfortunate that I left my beloved kin.
    Alas, I was deceived.

I had not gone far in my exploration
when I met a kind man

10 A thuirt rium, 'A fhleasgaich òig,
Dean suidhe còmhl' rium 'us leig d' anail.'

Thuirt e rium, 'us fiamh a' ghàir' air,
'Cuin a thàinig thu do 'n àite?
Am buin thu do chuideachd a'Mhàidseir
15 A thàinig Di-màirt do 'n chala?'

Thug e leis gu cùl-thaobh fàil mi
Shealltainn coille nach robh geàrrta;
'S mise 'm fear nach dean a h-àiteach,
Cha tugadh an Fhéinn aisd' aran.

20 A' chiad Di-dòmhnuich a b'fhaisge
Chaidh mi do'n t-searmon g'am faicinn;
Bha na mogaisean gu pailt ann.
Brògan cairte bha glé ainneamh.

'Na mo chridhe thuirt mi gu cianail,
25 'S bochd a dh'fhàg mi tìr na ciatachd
Thighinn a thàmh do 'n àird an iar seo
Ged bu mhiadhail mi air fearann.

'S ann a shaoil leam leis a'ghòraich'
'N uair a dh'fhalbh mi leis a'Chòirneal,
30 A bhi ann am spuir 's bhòtuinn
'Trusadh òir air bharr gach meangain.

Fhuair mi mach nach 'eil na cluaintean
'Tha fad as cho gorm 's a chualas;
Saoil sibh fhéin nach cùis ro chruaidh
35 Bhi call nan cluas le fuachd an earraich.

who said, 'Young lad,   10
sit down with me and rest a while.'

With a hint of a smile he said to me,
'When did you come here?
Are you one of the Major's company
who came to port on Tuesday?'   15

He led me over behind a brush fence
to show me the uncut forest;
I, for one, would not settle there,
for not even the Fingalians could wrest a livelihood from it.

On the following Sunday   20
I went to the service to see them [the congregation];
there were plenty of moccasins there,
but tanned shoes were very rare.

In my heart I said sorrowfully:
a pity I left the land of happiness   25
to come west to dwell here
even though I had wanted property.

In my folly I had thought
when I left with the Colonel,[6]
that I would be going about with spur and boot,   30
gathering gold from every treetop.

I soon discovered that far-away fields
are not so green as reported.
Imagine what a trying experience it is
to lose one's ears in the cold spring.   35

ORAN DO'N CHUAIRTEAR

Deoch slàinte Chuairtear a ghluais à Albainn,
Bho thìr nam mór-bheann 's a sheòl an fhairge,
Do'n dùthaich choilltich thoirt dhuinn a sheanachais,
'S am fear nach òl i, bidh móran feirg ris.

5   'N uair thig an Cuairtear ud uair 's a mhìos,
Gu'm bi na h-òganaich le toil-inntinn
A' tional eòlais bho chòmhradh sìobhalt,
'S bidh naigheachd ùr aige air cliù an sinnsear.

Gur lìonmhor maighdeann a th'ann an déidh air,
10 'S a bhios le caoimhneas a' faighneachd sgéil dheth;
Le solus choinnlean a bhios 'ga leubhadh,
'S bidh eachdraidh ghaoil aige do gach té dhiubh.

Cha'n ioghnadh òigridh thoirt moran spéis dha
'N uair tha na seann-daoin' tha call an léirsinn
15 'S an cinn air liathadh, cho dian an déidh air,
'S nach dean iad fhaicinn mur cleachd iad speuclair.

'S e 'n Cuairtear Gàidhealach an t-àrmunn dealbhach,
Le phearsa bhòidheach an comhdach balla-bhreac,
Mar chleachd a shìnnsear gu dìreadh gharbhlach,
20 'S e fearail, gleusda gu feum le armaibh.

'N uair thig e 'n tìr seo mu thìm na Samhna,
Bidh féileadh cuaiche mu chruachain theannta,
'S a bhreacan-guaille gu h-uallach, greannar;
Cha lagaich fuachd e no gruaim a'gheamhraidh.

25 Bidh boineid ghorm agus gearra-chòt ùr air,
Bidh osain dhealbhach mu chalpaibh dùmhail;
Bidh gartain stiallach thar fiar-bhréid cùil air,
'S a bhrògan éille, 's b'e 'n t-éideadh dùthchais.

A SONG FOR THE *TOURIST*

A toast to the *Tourist* who traveled from Scotland
and from the land of the mountains sailed across the sea
to this wooded country, to bring us his tidings.
He who will not toast him will be held in great contempt.

When that *Tourist* comes once a month,   5
the young people, with great enthusiasm,
will draw knowledge from his courtly conversation;
he brings them news about the fame of their ancestors.

Many a maiden hastens after him
and gently asks him for news.   10
By candlelight she regards him;
he has a love story for each one.

It is not surprising that the young are enamoured of him
when old people, with failing vision,
their heads turned grey, are so zealous about him,   15
even though they cannot see him without spectacles.

The Highland *Tourist* is a handsome hero
with his fine form and checkered garb,
like that of his forbears stalking the Highlands,
manly, alert, skilful with arms.   20

When he comes to this land at Halloween
a pleated kilt will gird him,
and his gay, handsome plaid will cover his shoulders;
neither cold nor the gloom of winter will daunt him.

He wears a blue bonnet and a new doublet,   25
fitted hose about his sturdy legs,
striped garters cross-tied behind,[7]
laced shoes, the full traditional dress.

Bidh lann gheur stàillinn 'n crios bhraiste airgiod air,
30 'S biodag dhualach de chruaidh na Gearmailt;
'Us dag air ghleusadh nach leum le cearbaich,
Le sporan iallach de bhian an t-seana-bhruic.

'S e sin an t-éideadh tha eutrom, uallach
Gu siubhal bheann agus ghleann 'us chruachan,
35 'S gu seasamh làraich an làthair cruadail;
Bu tric an nàmhaid an càs air ruaig leis.

'N uair chì mi an Cuairtear tha uasal, rìoghail,
Bidh mi 'g a shamhlachadh ri Iain Muilleir;
Tha fichead geamhradh bho'n tha e 's tìr seo,
40 'S cha d'fhuair e riamh air a shliasaid cuibhreach.

Tha còrr 'us ciad bho'n tha ciall 'us cuimhn' aig',
Is tric a shealg e damh dearg 's na frìthean
Air slios Beinn Armuinn a b'àrd ri dìreadh;
'S an déidh an t-seòrs' ud b'e 'n còmhlan fiachail.

45 'S a Chuairtear àlainn, tha 'tàmh 's na gleanntaibh,
'G a bheil a' Ghàidhlig 's as fheàrr a labhras i,
'S nach gabh tàmailt ge b'e ni sealltainn riut,
'S mòr de chàirdean tha 'n dràsd an geall ort.

Gu'n d'ghabh iad tlachd dhiot le beachd nach tréig iad,
50 Bho'n 's Gàidheal gasd' thu tha sgairteil, gleusda;
'S tu oighr' an Teachdaire chleachd bhith beusach,
'S cha d'fhàgadh masl' air a mhac na dhéidh leis.

'S a Chuairtear ghràdhaich, cha d'thugainn fuath dhuit;
Gu'n robh do chàirdeas ri sàr dhaoin'-uasal,
55 Ged rinn pàirt dhiubh do chàradh suarach,
A chaill an Gàidhlig, 's na s'fheàrr cha d'fhuair iad.

He wears a keen, steel sword in his studded silver belt,
and the traditional dirk of German metal, 30
together with loaded pistol which will not miss its mark,
and a leather sporran made from badger's skin.

This is the light, noble dress
in which to hunt among the bens, glens, and craigs,
and in which to stand firm in the face of hardship; 35
many a vanquished foe was routed by it.

When I see the courtly, regal *Tourist*,
I compare him to John the Miller;
the latter has been in this country twenty winters,
and his limbs have never been trammeled with foreign garb.[8] 40

His reason and memory have served him for more than a
thousand years,
Often did he hunt the red stag in the deer forest,
on the steep side of Beinn Armuinn;
hunting that kind [of game] was worth the climb.

Handsome *Tourist*, you who dwell in the glens 45
you know Gaelic, and you speak it best of all;
you are not ashamed of it, no matter what it may cost you.
Numerous are the friends who now support you.

They have derived satisfaction from you which they will not
relinquish,
for you are a stalwart, sturdy, handsome Gael; 50
you are the heir of the noble courier
and no reproach accrues to the son on that account.[9]

Beloved *Tourist*, I would not reject you;
your kinship is with illustrious men,
although some of them have treated you indifferently. 55
[They are] those who lost their Gaelic though they did not find
better.

'S i 'Ghàidhlig bhrìoghmhor bh'aig suinn na Féinne,
'S bu daoine calma nan aimsir féin iad.
'S rinn Oisein dànachd dhaibh air a réir sin;
60 'S gur h-i bh'aig Pàdruig a bheannaich Eirinn.

Gur mór na fiachan fo bheil na Gàidheil
Do'n fhear a dh'inntrich air leabhar nàduir,
'S a dhearbh le fìrinn gur h-i bh'aig Adhamh;
'S e bainne cìche a lìon gach cànain.

65 Bu lus bha prìseil i chinn 's a' ghàradh,
Bha'n stochd gun chrìonadh am brìgh 's an àilleachd;
'S cha robh ann siantan a mhìll a blàithean;
Bu ghlan gun truailleadh a fuaim an là sin.

A Chuairtear éibhinn, na tréig gu bràth i,
70 'S na leig air dìochuimhn' ri linn an àil s' i.
Bidh sinn 'ga seinn anns na coilltibh fàsaich
Mar bha Clann Israel a seinn am Bàb'lon.

'S a Chuairtear shìobhalt, ma ni thus m'iarrtas,
'S gu'n cuir thu 'n t-òran seo 'n clò nan iarann,
75 'Nad chaoimhneas giùlain do 'n chùrsa 'n iar e,
Do'n eilean ìosal, an tìr o'n thriall mi.

Am baile gaolach a' Chaolais àillidh
'S an robh mi còmhnaidh 'nam òige, fàg e,
Aig cnoc Mhic-Dhùghaill mu'n dlùth mo chàirdean;
80 'S thoir fios gu 'n ionnsuidh gu 'bheil mi 'm shlàinte.

'N uair bhios mi còmhla ri comunn càirdeil
'Nar suidhe còmhnard mu bhòrd taigh-thàirne,
Gu'n gabh mi 'n t-òran, gu'n òl, 's gum pàigh mi
Deoch-slàinte Chuairtear le buaidh do'n Ghàidhlig.

Gaelic was the rich language of the Fingalians,
and they were men of daring in their day;
Ossian composed fitting songs for them.
It was the language of Patrick who blessed Ireland.   60

The Gaels are greatly indebted
to him who investigated the origin legends
and truly proved that it was the language of Adam;[10]
every other tongue was nourished by its milk.

It was the fairest flower that grew in the Garden;   65
the stock did not decay either in substance or in beauty.
There were no storms to spoil its delicate blossoms;
clean and pure its sound at that time.

Comely *Tourist*, never neglect it
and do not let it be forgotten in this generation.   70
We sing it in these wild forests
as the Israelites sang it in Babylon.

And gentle *Tourist*, if you will carry out my wish
and publish this song in the press,
in your kindness bring it westward   75
to the lowly Isle from which I came.

In the dear township of beauteous Caolas,
where I dwelt as a youth, leave it
at MacDougall's hill where my kinsmen are numerous,
and tell them that I am in good health.   80

Whenever I am with cordial companions
sitting peacefully around the table in a tavern,
I'll sing a song, I'll drink, and I'll pay for
a toast to the *Tourist* and to the triumph of Gaelic.

John MacDonald / Iain Sealgair
(1795-1853)

John the Hunter MacDonald was born in the Braes of Lochaber in 1795. He sailed from Tobermory on the *Janet* and landed at Ship Harbour (now Port Hawkesbury), Cape Breton, in 1834.[1] His first winter in the New World was one of unusual severity, remembered long afterwards as 'geamhradh an t-sneachda mhóir' (winter of the big snow). He settled at Mabou Ridge, but he was never really happy there. He longed for the Highlands, the good company of old, and the delights of chasing the stag, all of which he had relinquished of his own will. Like many of his kinsmen, he had had great expectations of wealth and opportunity in

ORAN DO DH'AMERICA

Mo shoraidh bhuam an diugh air chuairt
Thar chuan do bhràigh' nan gleann,
Gu tìr nam buadh, ge fada bhuam i,
Tìr nam fuar bheann àrd.
5 'S e tigh'nn a thàmh do 'n àit s' as ùr
A dh'fhàg mo shùilean dall.
'N uair sheòl mi 'n iar, a' triall bho m' thìr,
A rìgh gur mi bha 'n call.

Dh' fhàg mi dùthaich, dh'fhàg mi dùthchas;
10 Dh'fhan mo shùgradh thall.
Dh'fhàg mi 'n t-àite bàigheil, caomh,
'S mo chàirdean gaolach ann.
Dh'fhàg mi 'n tlachd 's an t-àit' am faict' i,
Tìr nam bac 's nan càrn.
15 'S e fàth mo smaointinn bho nach d'fhaod mi
Fuireach daonnan ann.

America, but he found the climate disagreeable, life primitive, and the residents rude and intemperate. Like his contemporary, Bard Maclean, John the Hunter composed a number of songs in which he recorded his disenchantment. His bardic gift was hereditary, for he was related to the Bohuntin bards whose poetry was well known in Lochaber, and the poetic tradition continued in the line of his cousin, Allan the Ridge (see pages 81, 88-9), and the later Ridge MacDonalds. His song, *Oran do dh'America* (*Song for America*), alludes to most aspects of his early life in Scotland and ends with his dispirited observations about the 'land of heavy snows and sere grasses.'[2]

SONG FOR AMERICA

My greeting today over
across the ocean to the Braes [of Lochaber],
the land of heroes, far distant from me,
land of cold, high bens.
It was coming to dwell in this new world   5
that blinded my eyes.
When I sailed westward, leaving my country,
Lord, I did so at great loss.

I left my homeland, I left my heritage;
my joy was left behind.   10
I left the friendly, hospitable land,
and my beloved kinsmen there.
I left comfort and the place where it can be found,
the land of valleys and cairns.
I am now distressed because I did not choose   15
to remain there forever.[3]

Dh'fhàg mi cuideachda nam breacan
B' àlainn dreach 'us tuar;
Armuinn ghrinne, làidir, inich,
20 Gillean bu ghlan snuadh;
Fir chalma, reachdmhor, gharbh, 's iad tlachdmhor,
Bu dearg daite 'n gruaidh,
Luchd an fhéile 'n àm an fheuma
Leis an éireadh buaidh.

25 Bhiodh Dòmhnullaich 'nan éideadh gasd',
Cha cheum air ais bhiodh ann;
Luchd fhéile ghartan, chòtan tartain,
'S osain bhreac nam ball.
'S nam boineid ùra, dubh-ghorm, daite,
30 Air tùs am mach 'nan rang.
B'iad féin na seòid nach géill 's iad beò,
Bu treun 's a' chòmhrag lann.

'S tric a dhìrich mi ri màm
'S mo ghunna 'm làimh air ghleus,
35 Mo mhiann 's an àm bhith siubhal bheann
'S mo chuilein seang air éill;
Dìreadh ghlacagan 's a' gharbhlach,
Sealg air mac an fhéidh;
'S tric a leag mi e le m' luaidhe,
40 Ged bu luath a cheum.

Air maduinn chiùin bu mhiannach leam
Bhith falbh 's mo chù ri m'shàil,
Le m' ghunna dùbailte nach diùlt
'N uair chuirinn sùil ri h-eàrr.
45 Luaidhe 's fùdar 'chuir 'nan smùid,
'S i cheàird dh'an tug mi gràdh,
Feadh lùbaibh cam air àird nam beann
'S am bi damh seang a'fàs.

B'e siud m' aighear-sa 's mo shòlas
50 Crònanaich nam fiadh,

I left the tartaned company,
handsome of figure and mien;
trim warriors, elegant, strong,
lads of fresh countenance; 20
serene men, sturdy, able, and handsome,
high colour in their cheeks;
kilted hosts, in time of need
victory was assured them.

The MacDonalds would be in splendid array, 25
they were not wont to retreat;
the kilted gartered troop, with tartan coats,
and plaid hose to their heels,
with their new, dark blue bonnets,
always first in rank.[4] 30
Truly, they were gallant men who would never yield in life,
valiant in combat of swords.

Often did I climb through the pass
with my gun ready in hand.
It was my delight then to hunt among the bens 35
with my slender hound alert on the precipice,
roaming the dells on the wild moors,
stalking the young deer.
Often did I fell him with my lead
though swift his stride. 40

On a fine morning it was my delight
to set out with my dog at my heels,
with my double-barreled gun which would not fail
when I took aim.
To convert lead and gunpowder to smoke 45
was to me a pleasant pursuit,
among the winding trails on the mountain heights,
home of the slender stag.

My joy and my delight
were the bellowings of the deer, 50

Mu Fhéill-an-Ròid bhith tigh'nn a chòir
An fhir bu bhòidhche fiamh;
Bhith falbh nam bac 'gan sealg 's na glacaibh,
'N uair bu daite am bian.
55 'S tric a tholl mi mac na h-éilde
Seal mu'n éireadh grian.

A nis 's ann thréig gach cùis a bh'ann
Mi 'n seo 's mi 'm fang fo chìs
An tìr an t-sneachda 's nam feur seachte
60 Cha b'e a chleachd mi-fhìn;
A bhith faicinn dhaoine cairtidh,
Grannda, glas, gun bhrìgh,
Le triùsair fharsuinn, sgiùrsair casaig,
'S cha b'e 'm fasan grinn.

65 Chi thu còmhlan ac' ag òl
'S an stòr ma theid thu ann,
Iad ri bòilich 'us ri bòsd,
'S iad gòrach leis an dram;
An àite rapach, poll fo'n casan,
70 Stòpan glas ri 'n ceann,
Rùsgadh dheacaid dhiubh 's 'gan stracadh,
'S iad mar phaca cheàrd.

'S truagh, a Rìgh, gu'n d'chuir mi cùl
Ri m' dhùthaich le m' thoil fhìn,
75 Le bhith an dùil 's an àit' as ùr
Nach faicinn tùrn 'gam dhìth;
Ach còir air fearann, òr, 'us earras
Bhith aig gach fear a bh' innt'.
Bha chùis gu baileach òrm am falach,
80 'S mheall mo bharail mì.

Thug mise cion 'n uair bha mi òg
Do bhith an còir nam beann,
'Us saoilidh càch gu'n robh mi gòrach
'S gun iad eólach ann.

and at Holy Rood to approach
the one of fairest hue;[5]
to traverse the glades and hunt them on the moors,
when their pelts were darkest.
Many a time I riddled the young roe   55
before sunrise.

Now all that was has ceased to be;
I am bound, brought low,[6]
in the land of snows and sere grasses.
It is not what I have been accustomed to,   60
looking at swarthy folk,
ugly, drab, dull,
with wide trousers, the loutish long coat,
an unattractive style.

You'll see groups of them drinking   65
at the store if you go there.
They are rowdy and boastful,
intoxicated by drink;
their place untidy, mud under their feet,
glass flagons raised to their heads,   70
peeling off and tearing their jackets
like a pack of tinkers.

Alas, Lord, that I turned my back
on my country of my own free will,
thinking that in the new world   75
not a penny would I need;
rather a right to property, gold, and riches
would be the lot of everyone there.
The true state of affairs was hidden from me,
and my presumption deceived me.   80

In my youth I was fond of
frequenting the bens;
others may think that I was foolish,
but they are not acquainted there.

85 An spéis a thug mi dhamh na cròic
Cha téid ri m' bheò á m' chom;
Bho'n dh'fhàg mi tìr na seilg 's nan sàr
Tha m'aigneadh cràiteach, trom.

Cha chluinn mi dùrdan maduinn dhrùchd
90 Am barraibh dlùth nan sliabh;
Cha loisg mi fùdar gorm o'n stùc
'S cha chuir mi cù ri fiadh.
Bho'n chuir gach cùis a bh'ann rium cùl,
Dha'n tug mi rùn gu dian,
95 'S tìm dhomh bhith na's tric air m'ùrnaigh
'S leanachd dlùth ri Dia.

'S truagh, a Rìgh, nach robh mi marbh,
Mu'n d'fhàg mi Albainn thall,
Mu'n d'chuir mi cùl ri tìr mo rùin,
100 'S e dh'fhàg mo shùgradh mall;
Na'n gabhadh Dia ri m' anam bhuam
'S an uair cha robh mi 'n call,
'S mo chorp a thìodhlaiceadh 's an uaigh
A bh' air a'bhruaich 's a' ghleann.

105 Cille Choraill, Cill' as bòidhche
Air 'n d'chuir mi eòlas riamh;
Lagan bòidheach, grianail, còmhnard,
Far 'm bheil còmhnuidh chiad.
Tom nan aingeal, glac an Dòmhnuich,
110 'S an robh mo sheòrs' bho chian;
'S truagh, a Rìgh, gun mi 's a'chòmhlan
Mar bu deòn le m' mhiann.

My love for the antlered stag   85
will never leave me.
Since I left the land of the chase and gallant men,
my spirit is anguished, weary.

I do not hear murmuring on a dewy morning
in the thick mountain copse.   90
I do not shoot blue power from the ledge
nor set hound upon the deer.
Since all that used to be is no longer mine,
that which I always loved,
it is time for me to pray more often   95
and follow God more closely.

Alas, Lord, that I did not die
before I left Scotland,
before I turned my back on my dear homeland
and thereby lost my vigour.   100
If God had received my restless soul
at the time, I would not have suffered loss,
and my body would have been buried in the grave
on the heights above the glen,

at St Cairrail's churchyard, the most beautiful cemetery[7]   105
that I ever knew;
a pretty, sunny, smooth enclosure,
where hundreds now lie.[8]
Angels' Grove, Sunday's Dell,
where those of my kind have lain for years,   110
alas, Lord, that I am not among them
as I ardently long to be.

Allan MacDonald / Allan the Ridge
(1794-1868)

Allan MacDonald left the Braes of Lochaber in 1816.[1] As he crossed the perilous ocean, he thought of his friends at home and hoped that they would soon join him. He had little zest for living among 'yellow people and negroes.' He feared that he would never hear the cuckoo again; neither fruit nor birds were to be found in the great forests of America. Such were his preconceptions of the New World as set down in *Mi an toiseach na luinge* (*I am in the bow of the ship*) a song he composed at sea.[2] He survived the voyage across the Atlantic, but getting from Pictou across to Cape Breton in late October proved a hazardous venture. The shallop, hired to transport the newly arrived emigrants, met with a severe tempest which endangered all on board. They were forced to put ashore near Antigonish and reached their destination only the following summer.

The young bard took up residence at Mabou Ridge, and there acquired the patronymic borne by all of his descendants to this

CHUIR THU BOILICH SIOS 'US BOSD

Chuir thu bòilich sìos 'us bòsd
Air cùisean mór 'nad rann;
Searbh do ghlòir leam cainnt do bheòil
Oir bha mi eòlach thall,
5   An Albainn fhuar ge fada bhuam i
Suarach leam an call;
B' e fàth a' ghruaim an càradh cruaidh
Bh' air truaghain bhochd a bh' ann.

Fhuair na h-uaislean i dhaibh fhéin,
10   Gu'n éibhneas a chuir suas;

day. He moved to South River, Antigonish County, in 1847 and remained there until his death in 1868. Throughout his long life he maintained an active interest in his literary and historical heritage. The genealogies, tales, and songs of Lochaber were well known to him; indeed he and his son, Alexander, were authorities on the songs of Sìlis na Ceapaich (Juliet MacDonald), Iain Lom MacDonald, and many others.

Allan the Ridge was still living in Mabou when his cousin, John the Hunter, arrived from Scotland. By that time his attitude had mellowed greatly, and he was disposed to defend his new home and its residents. He refuted Iain Sealgair's song of dissatisfaction with a somewhat exaggerated portrayal of the good fortunes of the emigrant in *Chuir thu bòilich sìos 'us bòsd (You have been loud and boastful)*.[3] The song is a brave attempt to demonstrate that emigration opened the door to freedom and security, privileges which were now beyond the reach of hundreds of Highlanders in the old country.

YOU HAVE BEEN LOUD AND BOASTFUL

You have been loud and boastful
about many things in your song;
offensive to me is the utterance from your lips,
for I, too, knew conditions over there
in cold Scotland; though far from me,   5
I consider that no great loss.
A true cause of sorrow is the harsh treatment
endured by the poor people there

The nobles got it [the land] for themselves
to enhance their status;   10

Tha clann na tuath aca 'na sléibhean
Ann an éiginn chruaidh.
'S ged theid fear gu féill le breacan
Ann an dreach corr' uair,
15 'Chuid eile an tìm bidh e na chìleag
Sgàthach, dìblidh, truagh.

'S aobhar bròin do fhear a phòsas
'S e gun dòigh ann dhà,
Ach bean 'na h-aonar 's isean òg
20 Am bothan frògach, fàil.
Bidh e 'na ròmachan dubh, dòite,
Ag iomain dhròbh do chàch;
Bidh iadsan goirteach 's esan bochd
A' falbh le 'phocan bàn.

25 Ged 's mór do bhòsd à fear na cròic
Mu ni thu a leòn dhuit fhéin,
Ged is staoigeach, tioram' fheòil,
Bidh tòireachd as do dhéidh.
Theid breith air amhaich ort gu grad
30 'Us gad a chuir 'ad mhéill,
'Us d'fhògairt thar a' chuan air falbh
Chionn bhi sealg an fhéidh.

'S i 'n tìr a dh'fhàg thu 'n tìr gun chàirdeas,
Tìr gun bhàidh ri tuath;
35 Ach gu tùrsach iad 'ga fàgail
'S ànradh thar a' chuan.
Daoine bochda, sìol nan coiteir,
Bha gun stochd gun bhuar;
'S mairg a chàin i, tìr an àigh,
40 'S an dràsd' iad 'nan daoine uaisl'.

Nis bho'n thàinig thu thar sàile
Chum an àite ghrinn,
Cha bhi fàilinn ort ri d' là
'S gach aon nì fàs dhuinn fhìn.

they hold the sons of the tenantry as slaves
in dire need.
Although one may go to a festivity in the tartan,
properly dressed on occasion,
the rest of the time one is only a dupe,   15
timid, wretched, poor.

It is a cause of sorrow to one who marries
that he can only provide
for his lonely bride and young child
a dismal vacant hut.   20
He will be as a dark, singed caterpillar,
droving cattle for others.
They will be miserly, and he poor,
going about with his white sack.

Although you take great pride in the antlered one,   25
if you shoot him for yourself,
though his flesh be lean and dry,
you will be prosecuted.
You will be seized swiftly by the throat,
a lash to your face,   30
and you'll be exiled across the ocean
for hunting the deer.

The land you left is a land without kindness,
a land without respect for tenants;
they are sorrowful leaving it,   35
fearing the stormy seas.
Poor people, sons of cotters,
without stock or herd –
it is not fitting to dispraise the land of promise
where they are now respected men.   40

Now that you have come across the sea
to this fair land,
you will want for nothing the rest of your life;
everything prospers for us.

45 Gheibh thu mil air bharr nan lusan,
Siùcar agus tì;
'S fheàr dhuit siud no'n tìr a dh'fhàg thu
Aig a' ghràisg 'na frìth.

'S tu rinn glic 's nach deach am mearachd
50 'S cha robh do bharail faoin;
Tighinn do dhùthaich na fear glana,
Coibhneal, tairis, caomh.
Far a faigh tu òr a mhaireas,
Còir air fearann saor,
55 Gach nì bu mhath leat bhi mu d' bhaile,
Earras 'us crodh laoigh.

Gheibh thu ruma, fìon 'us beòir,
'S an stòr ma theid thu ann.
Chì thu còmhlan dhaoine còire,
60 'S iad ag òl 's an àm;
Daoine dàna, fearail, fialaidh,
Riaraicheas an dràm;
Gach fear dhiubh triall air each le dhìollaid
'S bu mhiann leam bhi 'nan ceann.

John MacQueen
(1809-1835)

One of the lesser known Skye bards was the young John Mac-
Queen,[1] whose song, *C'àit' an caidil an nionag an nochd* (*Where will
the young girl sleep tonight?*), is still very popular in Gaelic-speaking communities. According to a Cape Breton tradition, John
was the son of Donald Og MacQueen. He was born in Troternish
and moved with his family to Kilmuir in 1824. There he met and
courted Catherine Beaton, the subject of his song. His parents
objected vehemently to the courtship on grounds of social

You'll get honey from the flowers,   45
sugar and tea;
better that than the land you left
with the rabble in charge of its forests.

You acted wisely and were not deceived;
your judgment was not in error   50
when you came to the land of the righteous,
the kind, the trustworthy, the gentle,
where you'll get lasting wealth,
a right to free land,
everything you would wish to have in your home,   55
riches, and herds of cattle.

You'll get rum, wine, and beer
in the store if you go there.
You'll see a company of gentlemen
drinking there as well;   60
courageous, hardy, generous men,
who will share the dram.
Each of these goes about on his saddle horse;
would that I were among them.

---

inequality. Around 1829 Catherine emigrated with her family to
Cape Breton. The young bard was determined to follow her, but
again his parents intervened; it is said that they had him bound,
hand and foot, to restrain him. Ironically, after his untimely
death in 1835, his father and mother and several of their children went out to Cape Breton.

   C'àit' an caidil an nìonag an nochd is the poignant cry of one
who was treated heartlessly by his family and deprived forever

of his sweetheart through emigration. Other Gaelic songs record similar disappointments, but it is unlikely that they were inspired by identical circumstances.[2] MacQueen's song has been pub-

---

C'AIT' AN CAIDIL AN NIONAG AN NOCHD

An uair a dh'fhàg an long an cala
Bha mo leannan fhìn innt';
'Us b'e mo mhiann bhith air na tonnaibh
Far an robh mo nìonag.

5   O, c'àit' an caidil an nìonag an nochd?
O, c'àit' an caidil an nìonag?
Far an caidil an nìonag an nochd,
Is truagh nach robh mi fhìn ann.

An uair a thog iad rithe siùil
10 Bha mise tùrsach, cianail,
'Us shuidh mi air a' chnoc a b'àirde
Gus an d'fhàg i m'fhianais.

Is truagh nach robh mi 'measg nam ball
Ri bàrr nan crann a' dìreadh;
15 'S gum faighinn sealladh de mo luaidh
Air druim a'chuain ged bhìodhmaid.

'S ann agam fhìn bha nìonag òg
Bu bhòidhche bha 's an tìr seo;
A deud mar chailc, a gruaidh mar ròs,
20 'S a pòg air bhlas an fhìona.

Cha robh duin' uasal bha mu'n cuairt
A chunnaic snuadh mo nìonaig,
Nach robh an geall air deanamh suas
Ri bean a' chuailein rìomhaich.

lished in many collections, journals, and newspapers. The most complete text is that in *Mac-Talla*, edited here.[3] It is a fine song in the original but loses much of its force and poetic quality in translation.

WHERE WILL THE YOUNG LASS SLEEP TONIGHT?

When the vessel left the shore
my sweetheart was on board;
I yearned to be at sea
with my young lass.

   O, where will the young lass sleep tonight?   5
   O, where will the young lass sleep?
   Where she sleeps tonight
   would that I were there.

When they unfurled the sails
I was sad and lonely;   10
I sat on the highest hill
Until she had disappeared from sight.

Alas, that I am not among the crew
climbing to the top of the mast;
I'd get a glimpse of my beloved   15
though far out at sea.

My sweetheart
was the fairest in this land;
her teeth like chalk, her cheek like the rose,
her kiss like the taste of wine.   20

There was not a young man
who, on seeing my sweetheart's beauty,
did not resolve to court
this lady of the fair tresses.

25 Is ann ort fhéin a dh'fhàs a'ghruag,
Tha buidhe, dualach, fìnealt';
Air dhreach an òir as bòidhche snuadh
'Na dhualaibh troimh na cìribh.

Ged bheirteadh dhomhsa na tha do dh'òr
30 'S an Olaint 's anns na h-Innseabh,
Gu'm b' annsa leam bhith 'n nochd a' seòladh
Còmhla ri mo nìonaig.

Is mi tha diombach dhe mo bhràithrean,
'S dhe mo chàirdean dìleas,
35 A chum air ais mi gun do phòsadh
'S tu cho bòidheach, fìnealt'.

Cha toir guth binn nan teud no òran,
'S cha toir ceòl na pìoba,
'S cha toir té a théid 'na còmhdach
40 Air mo bhròn-sa dìobradh.

Ann seo ma dh'fhàgas mis' am bliadhna
Fiachaidh mi le dìchioll,
'Us seòlaidh mi amach à Grianaig
No à bialaibh Lìte.

45 Theid mi do thìr nan coilltean mòra,
'S gheibh mi pòg bho m' nìonaig;
'N sin teichidh m' airsneal 'us mo bhròn,
'Us tillidh sòlas crìdh' rium.

Kenneth MacDonald
(dates unknown)

Kenneth MacDonald is not as well known as his contemporaries,
Bard Maclean and John the Hunter MacDonald.[1] A native of

You were the one with hair   25
so fair, beautiful, elegant,
golden, of finest beauty,
in tresses held with combs.

Although I should be given all the gold
in the Orient and the Indies,   30
I would prefer to be sailing tonight
with my sweetheart.

I am resentful towards my brothers
and towards my close relatives,
who prevented me from marrying you,   35
the beautiful, graceful one.

Not the sweet sound of strings or voice,
nor the music of the pipes,
and no one who may take her place
can lessen my sorrow.   40

If I should leave here this year
I'll work earnestly,
and I'll sail from Greenock
or from the mouth of the Leith.

I'll go to the land of great forests,   45
and there I'll get a kiss from my sweetheart;
then my gloom and sadness will vanish,
and joy will fill my heart again.

Gairloch, he emigrated to Cape Breton in 1842 and settled on Big
Island (Boularderie). The bitter cold and deep snow caused him to

regret that he had ever left the country. He would gladly have sold his cattle after the first winter and returned to Gairloch. Spring must have brought him new hope, for he remained at Big Island the rest of his life, and his widow and family were still there in 1901. Although the Bras d'Or region received many Highland emigrants in the first half of the nineteenth century, Kenneth Mac-

---

ORAN DO AMERICA

Tha Ceap Breatunn seo cho fuar
Reòthadh e na cluasan fhéin;
Theid e cho domhain 's an tuaigh
'S i 'n lasair a dh'fhuasglas innt' e.

5   Bheir mi ho air Mòrag ho,
Hiuthaill ho air Mòrag fhéin,
Dh'fhalbhainn-sa le Mòrag ho,
Thogainn fonn 's gu'n ceann'chinn spréidh.

Mogais chaisionn air an t-sluagh,
10   'Gan cumail bho 'n fhuachd gu léir,
'Gan gearradh á seiche chruaidh
'S 'gam fuaigheal umpa le éill.

'N uair a thig an còta bàn
Falaichidh e na màgain fhéin;
15   Fuirichidh e leth bhliadhna slàn,
'S bidh 'n talamh 'na thàmh gun fheum.

America a'chòta bhàin,
B'fheàrr leam a bhi 'n Geàrrloch fhéin,
Far 'm biodh earrach agus Màrt,
20   'S far am biodh am blàths 's a' ghréin.

Chan eil ianlaith anns an àit'
Ach seòrsachan a dh'fhàs ann fhéin;

Donald seems to have been one of the few bards who recorded in song the rigours of pioneer life there.[2] His *Oran do America* (*Song for America*) is very much like some of the compositions of Bard Maclean, by whom he was probably influenced.[3] The song is a vivid description of the debilitating effects of the frigid winter as well as an interesting commentary on the unusual birds and wild life around Boularderie at that time.

SONG FOR AMERICA

Cape Breton is so cold
that one's very ears will freeze;
it [the frost] penetrates the axe so deeply
that only fire can thaw it out.

I will with Morag ho   5
Hiuthaill ho with Morag herself,
I would go with Morag ho;
I would sing and buy a herd.

People wear white-soled moccasins
to protect them from the cold;   10
these are cut from a stiff hide
and sewn up with thong.

When the white blanket comes,
it will conceal all ground beasts;
it will stay for a full half year   15
while the land remains dormant.

America, the white-coated,
I would much prefer to be in Gairloch,
where spring comes in March
with real warmth in the sun.   20

There is no fowl in this place
except the native species;

Gròbair-coill' 's a ghob an còis
'G iarraidh àite-seòin dha fhéin.

25 Coinean agus madadh-ruadh,
Ar leam gur h-uamhasach iad;
'S na 'm faiceadh tu an fheòrag-ruadh
Gur a h-ise 's luaithe ceum.

Na 'm faighinn reic air a' chrodh ruadh
30 Ghabhainn soitheach luath a réisd;
Rachainn a null thar a' chuan
'S dh'fhàgainn am fuachd aca fhéin.

Duncan Black Blair
(1815-1893)

Duncan Black Blair was born at Strachur in Cowal in 1815.[1] He
entered the University of Edinburgh in 1834, but his studies
were interrupted by illness in 1837. In the following year he
went to Skye where he tutored the children of Malcolm Nichol-
son of Ulinish. In 1844 he received his license to preach from
Divinity Hall, Edinburgh, and two years later he emigrated to
Nova Scotia, where he became minister at Barney's River and
Blue Mountain, Pictou County. Thus began his long association
with the unusual Gaelic literary tradition of that area, fostered

BRAIGH' ABHAINN BHARNAIDH

Thig an àird' leam gu Bràigh'
Abhainn Bhàrnaidh do'n choille;
Far am fàs an subh làir,
'S cnothan làna gun ghainne.
5 An lon àrd bidh 'na uaill
'Gabhail cuairt ann gu loinneil,

the woodpecker with his beak in a crevice
seeking a feast for himself.

The rabbit and the red fox   25
seem strange to me;
if you could see the red squirrel –
it is the swiftest of all.

If I could sell my red cattle,
I would then take a swift ship;   30
I would cross the ocean
and leave the cold to themselves.

---

for many years by clerical and lay scholars. His own Gaelic
works reflected a wide range of interests from metrical translations of the Psalms to the awesome roar of Niagara Falls.

Dr Blair had the distinction of officiating at the marriage of the
Reverend Alexander Maclean Sinclair on 1 August 1882. A few
years later he composed *Bràigh' Abhainn Bharñaidh* (*Upper Barney's
River*). Unlike the anguished cry of many an emigrant, this song is
an invitation to partake of the natural riches of Barney's River
and to share the good fellowship and comfort which help to
while away the long cold winters.[2]

UPPER BARNEY'S RIVER

Come with me to Upper
Barney's River in the forest,
where strawberries grow
and an abundance of ripe nuts.
The tall moose very proudly   5
makes his circuit with elk-like grace;

'S bidh an fheòrag le srann
Null 's a nall feadh a dhoirean.

Gheibhear fìor-uisg' nach truaill
10 Anns na fuaranaibh fallain,
Agus àile glan, ùr,
Feadh nam flùr 'us a' bharraich.
Bheir sinn sgrìob feadh nan stac,
Feadh nan glac 's nan gleannan;
15 'S bidh sinn sòlasach, ait,
Leis gach taitneas 'nar sealladh.

Anns a' gheamhradh neo-chaoin
Thig a' ghaoth le fead ghoineant';
'S bidh cruaidh ghaoir feadh nan craobh,
20 'S iad fo shraonadh na doinnin.
Bidh sneachd trom air gach gleann,
'S cathadh teann mu gach dorus;
Ach bidh lòn againn 's blàths,
'S bidh sinn mànranach, sona.

25 Thig na h-eòin le'n ceòl réidh,
'N uair a dh'éireas an t-earrach;
Theid an geamhradh air chùl
Agus dùdlachd na gaillionn.
Bidh gach ailein 'us cluain
30 'Sealltainn uain'-fheurach, maiseach,
'S bidh gach creutair fo àgh
'Us am blàths tigh'nn air ais uc'.

Thig an samhradh mu'n cuairt
Chuireas snuadh air an fhearann;
35 Cinnidh blàthan a' Mhàigh
Agus neòineanan geala
Aig Loch Bhrura an àigh,
Air gach àird agus bealach.
Bidh sinn aoibhneach gach là
40 Ma bhios slàinte m'ar teallach.

the squirrel whizzes
back and forth among its thickets.

There is fresh, pure water
in the nourishing springs, 10
and a fresh, clean scent
among the flowers and the brushwood.
We'll take a stroll among the hills
through the glades and glens,
and we'll be cheerful, gay, 15
with every pleasure before us.

In the harsh winter
the wind is shrill and piercing;
a howling moan whistles through the trees,
lashed by tempests. 20
There is deep snow in every valley
and drifts at every door;
but we have food and comfort,
and we are contented, happy.

Birds return with their sweet melodies 25
when spring unfolds;
winter disappears
and the dreariness of the gales.
Each meadow and plain
appears green, beautiful; 30
all creatures thrive
as warmth returns to them.

Summer comes
to adorn the land;
mayflowers blossom, 35
and white daisies
at delightful Loch Brura,[3]
and on each hill, in every glen.
We are happy each day
if there be health at our hearth. 40

3 Prince Edward Island

Calum Bàn MacMhannain
(1758-1829)

Lord Selkirk's colonizing venture in Prince Edward Island has been documented in considerable detail, both by Selkirk and by later historians. A significant supplementary record was provided by the illiterate bard, Calum Bàn MacMhannain,[1] an emigrant who sailed to the Island on the *Polly* in August 1803. Calum Bàn spent his early years at Sarsdal in Flodigarry on the Isle of Skye. There is some evidence that he was in fair circumstances there, but the extortions of the bailie and intermittent plague among his cattle induced him to emigrate. Presumably his wife and six children accompanied him to the Island. There he settled at Point Prim near other Selkirk colonists.

Calum Bàn knew the shores of his native Skye with an intimacy typical of Hebrideans. Moreover, he was keenly attuned to the sounds and signs of impending storms and to the hazards of sailing. For him the initial stages of the voyage from Portree around the north coast of Skye were a stirring adventure. No other Highland emigrant recorded this kind of experience in such detail as he did in his song, *Imrich nan Eileineach (Emigration of the Islanders)*. The song is of interest in other respects too. The bard makes illuminating remarks about the changing conditions in Skye and the general disregard for the tenantry, which necessitated emigration. He advised his compatriots that they will prosper if they come to Prince Edward Island, the land of plenty.[2]

IMRICH NAN EILEINEACH

An àm togail dhuinn fhìn
Mach o Chala Phortrìgh
'S iomadh aon a bh'air tìr 's iad brònach;
Iad ag amharc gu dlùth
5 Null 's an sùil air an luing,
'S ise 'gabhail a null gu Rònaidh.
Thuirt Mac Faid as an Dìg,
'S e ag éigheach rium fhìn,
''S ann a laigheas i sìos gu Trodaidh,
10 'S biodh am fear as fheàrr tùr
Nis 'na shuidh' air an stiùir,
Gus an teid i os cionn as t-Soain.

Eilean eil' ann da réir
Agus Sgeir na Ruinn Géir,
15 'S bidh muir air a' bhéisd an còmhnuidh;
Tha cnap eil' ann no dhà,
'S ann dhiubh sin Clach nan Ràmh,
'S Bogha Ruadh, tha fo Aird 'Ic Thorlain;
Leachd-na-Buinne seo shuas,
20 'S Rubha 'n Aiseig ri 'cluais,
Mol-a-Mhaide 's e cruaidh le dòirneig.
Thoir an aire gu dlùth
Cumail àrd os an cionn;
Seachain sruth Rubha Hunais, 's mór e.'

25 Dh'éirich soirbheas o'n tuath
Dhuinn os cionn Fladaidh-chuain,
'S ann a ghabhadh i 'n uair sin òran;
I a' siubhal gu luath,
'S i a' gearradh ma cluais,
30 'Dol a ghabhail a' chuain 's i eòlach.
Thug mi suil as mo dhéidh
Null air Rubh' a' Chàirn Leith,

EMIGRATION OF THE ISLANDERS

When we set out
from the harbour at Portree
there were many sorrowful people on shore;
they gazed across intently
with their eye on the vessel   5
as she headed for Rona.[3]
Said MacFadyn from Digg
as he shouted to me,
'She will veer down towards Trodday;
let the most skillful   10
be at the helm
until she reaches beyond Soain.

There is another island also
and Sgeir na Ruinn Geir,
which is usually concealed by the sea.   15
There is another obstacle or two:
among these Clach nam Ramh
and Bodha Ruadh under Aird 'ic Thorlain,
Leachd-na-Buinne up yonder[4]
And Rubha na h-Aiseig adjacent to it,   20
Mol-a-Mhaide with its hard-set boulder.
Be very careful
to keep well above these;
avoid Rubha Hunish with its strong current.'

A north wind arose   25
when we were above Fladda-Chuain;
then she hummed along
moving rapidly
as she tacked around
to take the main she knew so well.   30
I glanced behind me
towards Rubh' a' Chàirn Leith

'Us cha'n fhaca mi fhìn ach ceò air.
Sin 'n uair labhair MacPhàil,
35 'S e ag amharc gu h-àrd,
''S mór mo bheachd gur h-e bàrr a' Stòir e.'

Moire, 's minig a bha
Mise treis air a sgàth
Ann an Rig, 's gu'm b'e 'n t-àite bhó e!
40 'N uair a thigeadh am Màrt,
Bhiodh an crodh anns a' Chàrn,
'S bhiodh na luibhean co-fhàs ri neòinean.
Bhiodh an luachair ghorm ùr,
Nìos a' fàs anns a' bhùrn,
45 Fo na bruthaichean cùbhra, bòidheach;
Bhiodh na caoraich da réir
Ann ri mire 's ri leum,
'S iad a' breith anns a' Chéit uain' òga.

Thàinig maighstir as ùr
50 Nis a stigh air a' ghrunnd,
Sin an naigheachd tha tùrsach, brònach.
Tha na daoine as a' falbh,
'S ann tha 'm maoin an déigh searg';
Chan 'eil mart aca dh'fhalbhas mòinteach.
55 Chuireadh cuid dhiubh 's a' mhàl,
'S fhuair cuid eile dhiubh 'm bàs,
'S tearc na dh'fhuirich a làthair beò dhiubh.
Ciod a bhuinnig dhomh fhìn
Bhi a' fuireach 's an tìr,
60 O nach coisinn mi nì air brògan.

'S ann a theid mi thar sàil,
'S ann a leanas mi càch,
Fiach a faigheamaid àite còmhnuidh.
Gheibh sinn fearann as ùr,
65 'S e ri cheannach a grunnd,
'S cha bhi sgillinn ri chùnntas oirnn dheth.
'S math dhuinn fasgadh nan craobh,

and saw only mist over it.
Then MacPhail spoke
as he gazed upwards,   35
'I do believe it is the top of Storr.'

By Mary, how often
did I spend time in its shade
in Rigg; it was an ideal place for cattle.
When March came   40
there would be cattle in Carn,
and grasses grew with the flowers.
Fresh new rushes
grew deep in the burn
under the fragrant, pretty banks.   45
The sheep likewise
were there, sporting and leaping,
giving birth to young lambs in early May.

A new master has come
into the land,   50
a said, woeful matter.
The people are leaving;
their possessions have dwindled.
They haven't a cow to put to graze.
Some were put towards rent,   55
others died;
rare were those that survived.
What would it profit me
to remain in this land
where I can earn nothing by shoemaking.   60

I'll go to sea;
I'll follow others
in search of a place to dwell.
We'll get new land
which can be bought outright,   65
and we'll not be charged a shilling for it [afterwards].
Better for us the shelter of the forest

Seach na bruthaichean fraoich,
Bhiodh a muigh ann an aodann Ghròbain.
70 Air na leacan lom, fuar,
'N uair a thigeadh am fuachd,
Sin an t-astar bu bhuaine mòinteach.

Moire, 's fhada dhuinn fhìn
Rinn sinn fuireach 's an tìr,
75 Ged a thogamaid nì gu leòir ann;
'S iomadh dosgainn 'us call
Thigeadh orra 'nan àm
Chuireadh seachad feadh bheann ri ceò iad.
Ged a rachmaid gu féill
80 'S ged a reiceamaid treud
'S ged a gheibheamaid feich gu leòir air,
Thig am Bàillidh mu'n cuairt
Leis na sumanaidh chruaidh,
'S bheir e h-uile dad uainn dheth còmhla.

85 B'e sin fitheach gun àgh
Tha air tighinn an dràsd',
'S e 'n a Bhàillidh an àite 'n Leòdaich;
Umaidh àrdanach, cruaidh,
'S e gun iochd ris an tuath,
90 E gun taise, gun truas, gun tròcair.
'S beag an t-ìoghnadh e fhéin
Bhi gun chàirdeas fo'n ghréin,
Oir chan aithne dhomh fhéin có 's eòl dha,
Ach an Caimbeulach ruadh
95 O thaobh Asainn o thuath;
'S nam bu fada fear buan dheth sheòrsa.

Ach ma theid thu gu bràth
A null thairis air sàil,
Thoir mo shoraidh gu càirdean eòlach.
100 Thoir dhaibh cuireadh gun dàil
Iad a theicheadh o'n mhàl,
'S iad a thighinn cho tràth 's bu chòir dhaibh.

than the heather-covered hills
facing towards Grobainn.
On the bare, forbidding rocks,   70
when the cold weather came
the moorland seemed endless.

By Mary, for a very long time
we remained in that land;
although we could raise sufficient [provisions] there,   75
many a calamity and loss
plagued these at times,
so that they vanished into the mists on the mountain.
Although we might go to market
and sell our herd,   80
for which we got a fair price
the bailie would come around
with the cruel summons
and extort the entire sum from us.

It is a miserable vulture   85
who has come to us now
as bailie instead of MacLeod;[5]
a haughty, harsh brute
without clemency for the tenantry,
without compassion, pity, or mercy.   90
Small wonder that he, himself,
has no friends under the sun;
I know no one who is acquainted with him
except Red Campbell
from North Assynt;[6]   95
and may his kind be short-lived.

But if you ever go
over the sea
bring my greetings to my friends.
Urge them without delay   100
to flee the rents
and come out as soon as opportune for them.

'Us nam faigheadh iad àm
'S dòigh air tighinn a nall,
105 'N sin cha bhiodh iad an taing MhicDhòmhnuill;
'S ann a gheibheadh iad àit'
Anns an cuireadh iad bàrr,
'S ro-mhath chinneadh buntàta 's eòrn' ann.

'S e seo Eilean an àigh
110 Anns a bheil sinn an dràsd'
'S ro-mhath chinneas dhuinn blàth air pòr ann.
Bidh an coirc' ann a' fàs
Agus cruithneachd fo bhlàth,
Agus tuirneap 'us càl 'us pònair.
115 Agus siùcar nan craobh
Ann ri fhaighinn gu saor,
'S bidh e againn 'na chaoban móra;
'S ruma daite, dearg, ùr,
Anns gach bothan 'us bùth,
120 Cheart cho pailt ris a' bhùrn 'ga òl ann.

Rory Roy MacKenzie
(1755- ?)

Rory Roy MacKenzie may have been a fellow passenger of Calum Bàn MacMhannain on the *Polly*, for he too was one of the Earl of Selkirk's colonists.[1] Tradition affirms that he was the hereditary chieftain of the MacKenzies of Applecross, but, possibly because his descent from John 2nd of Applecross could no⸀ be established with certainty, he did not succeed to the title.

The Selkirk Papers indicate that by 1807 Rory Roy was in possession of 250 acres in lot 58 at Pinette, Prince Edward Island. He had bought the land for 5 shillings an acre and made a payment of £32/18/1 in advance.[2] Two years later he sold the property to Charles Stewart and subsequently took up residence in the Fox

113 Rory Roy MacKenzie

If they could find a time
and means to come over
they would not be beholden to MacDonald.[7]   105
They would get land
in which to sow crops,
and potatoes and barley would grow very well there.

This is the isle of contentment
where we are now.   110
Our seed is fruitful here;
oats grow
and wheat, in full bloom,
turnip, cabbage, and peas.
Sugar from trees   115
may be had free here;
we have it in large chunks.
There is fresh red rum
in every dwelling and shop,
abundant as the stream, being imbibed here.   120

Harbour area of Cumberland County, Nova Scotia. After the
death of his first wife, Catherine Kennedy, who had emigrated
with him, he decided to return to Scotland, but serious illness
overtook him at Harwood Hills, Pictou County. There he met
and married his second wife, who was known as 'Jack MacKenzie,' and returned to the Gulf Shore where he spent the rest of
his life. The Public Records of Nova Scotia indicate that he was
buried in the MacKenzie cemetery at Pugwash, Cumberland
County, but the dates of his birth and death are not recorded.[3]
   Rory Roy was considered a fine bard, but it is hard to trace any
of his songs today. *An Imrich* (*The Emigration*) was composed on

the eve of his departure from Scotland.[4] He had been harassed by overlords; sheep were moving in as men were being moved out. The country would become a desert, open to invasion and conquest if Napoleon should come. Shepherds would not be able to

---

AN IMRICH

Ma 's e Selkirk na bàighe
Tha ri àite thoirt dhuinn,
Tha mi deònach, le m' phàisdean,
Dhol gun dàil air na tuinn.
5   Siud an imrich tha feumail
Dhol 'nar leum as an tìr s'
Do dh'America chraobhach,
'S am bi saors' agus sìth.
    Faigh an nall dhuinn am botul,
10   Thoir dhuinn deoch as mu'n cuairt;
'S mise a' fear a tha deònach
A'dhol a sheòladh a' chuain;
A'dhol a dh'ionnsaidh an àite
Gus 'n do bharc am mór-shluagh;
15   A'dhol gu Eilein Naomh Màiri,
'S cha bhi màl 'ga thoirt bhuainn.

A dheagh Aonghais Mhic-Amhlaidh,
Tha mi 'n geall ort ro mhór,
Bho'n a sgrìobh thu na briathran
20   'Us an gnìomh le do mheòir,
Gu'n grad chuir thu gu'r n-ionnsaidh
Long Ghallda nan seòl,
'Us ruith-chuip air a clàraibh
Thar nam bàrc-thonn le treòir.

25   Seo a' bhliadhna tha sàraicht'
Do dh'fhear gun àiteach, gun sunnd,

defend it. Notwithstanding these gloomy reflections, the bard
faced the long voyage to America with courage and envisioned
his new home as a land of bounty for strong, ambitious emigrants.

THE EMIGRATION

If it be the benign Selkirk
who will grant us a place,
with my children I am eager
to sail without delay.
It is necessary to emigrate,   5
to leave this land immediately,
and go to wooded America
where there will be freedom and peace.
  Bring us the bottle,
  pass a drink around to us;   10
  I am most eager
  to set sail across the sea,
  and to go to the place
  from which many have embarked;
  to go to St Mary's Isle,⁵   15
  and no rents will be exacted from us.

Now, worthy Angus Macaulay,⁶
I will wager
that since you wrote the instructions
and their terms with your own hands,   20
you will soon send us
a foreign vessel,
foam on her deck,
rushing powerfully over the waves.

This is a taxing year   25
for one without a dwelling, without cheer,

'N uair théid càch 's a' mhìos Mhàrta
Ris an àiteach le sùrd,
Tha luchd-riaghlaidh an àite
30 Nis 'gar n-àicheadh gu dlùth,
'S gur h-e an stiùir a thoirt an iar dhi
Nì as ciataiche dhuinn.

Ma 's e réiteachan chaorach
'N àite dhaoine bhios ann,
35 Gu'm bi Albainn an tràth sin
'S i 'na fàsaich do 'n Fhraing.
'N uair thig *Bonipart'* stràiceil
Le làimh làidir an nall,
Bidh na cìobairean truagh dheth
40 'Us cha chruaidh leinn an call.

'S mo ghuidhe ma sheòlas sinn
Gu'n deònaichear dhuinn
Gu'm bi 'n Tì uile ghràs-mhor
Dh' oidhch' 's a' là air ar stiùir,
45 Gu ar gleidheadh 's ar teàrnadh
Bho gach gàbhadh 'us cùis,
'S gu ar tabhairt làn sàbhailt
Do thìr àghmhor na mùirn.

Gheibh sinn fearann 'us àiteach
50 Anns no fàsaichean thall;
Bidh na coillteau 'gan rùsgadh
Ged bhiodh cùinneadh oirnn gann.
'N dràsd 's ann tha sinn 'nar crùban
'M bothain ùdlaidh gun taing,
55 'Us na bailtean fo chaoraich
Aig luchd-maoine gun dàimh.

Bidh am bradan air linne
'S cha bhi cion air na féidh;
Bidh gach eun air na crannaibh

when in March others go
to their ploughing eagerly.
The overlords here
reject us completely.   30
To turn the rudder westward
is the most sensible course for us.

If it be sheep-walks
which will replace men,
Scotland will then   35
become a wasteland for France.
When the arrogant Bonaparte comes
with his heavy hand,
the shepherds will be badly off,
and we will not grieve for them.   40

It is my wish, if we sail,
that it may be granted us
that the all merciful one
guide us night and day,
to save us and protect us   45
from every peril and need,
and to bring us safely
to the land of good cheer.

We shall get land and a home
in the wilderness yonder;   50
the forests will be cleared
though money will be scarce.
Now we are cramped
in gloomy huts without recompense,
and the fields are occupied by sheep   55
owned by the unfriendly rich.

There will be salmon in the lake,
and deer will not be wanting;
birds of every kind

60   Ann am barraibh nan geug;
Bidh an cruinneachd a' fàs dhuinn
'S bidh an t-àl aig an spréidh.
Ma bhitheas againn ar slàinte
Cha bhi càs oirnn no éis.

A MacLean Bard from Raasay
(dates unknown)

The only information about this obscure bard appears to be a brief
biographical note which was contributed to *Mac-Talla* in 1898
with the song, *Gearain air America* (*Complaint about America*).[1]
This note is a fitting introduction to the bard and to his song. It
typifies the usual form of introduction to Gaelic poetry preserved through oral tradition:

Fhuair mi an t-òran seo bho bheul-aithris mac de'n fhear a rinn e,
maille ri iomadh òran math eile a rinn e air dha tighinn do'n
dùthaich seo bho chionn trì fichead bliadhna air ais à Eilean
Ratharsaidh. 'S e duine còir, fìrinneach a bh'ann, agus maille ri
nithean eile nach robh a'tighinn ri chàileachd, tha e coltach nach
robh luchd na Beurla a' faotainn àite cho blàth 'na chridhe 's a
gheibheadh luchd na Gàidhlig. B'e 'Cunnard' a b' uachdaran air an
fhearann agus b'e 'Peters' a b'fhear-ionaid dha; agus bha a coltach gu
robh iac ie 'chéile an-iochdmhor. Agus ma bhios sibh cho math
agus an t-òran seo a chuir 's a' *Mhac-Talla*, 's gu'n còrdadh e ribh

GEARAIN AIR AMERICA

'S muladach a tha mi
'M *Murray Harbour* 's mi gun Bheurl';
Cha b' ionnan 's mar a b'àbhaist domh
Oir chleachd mi 'Ghàidhlig fhéin.

will perch on the treetops;   60
wheat will grow for us,
and the herd will bear their young.
If we have our health
we shall not be in want or distress.

---

fhéin 's ri cuid do luchd-leughaidh *Mhac-Talla*, ma dh'fhaoidte
gu'm faodainn tuilleadh dhiu fhaotainn. Cha deach gin dhe chuid
òrain a sgrìobhadh, agus saoilidh mi gu'm b'olc an airidh sin. 'S e
duine còir a bha fo dheagh chliù a bh'ann. 'S e 'am Bàrd MacIllea-
thain a bh'air a' bhruaich a chainte ris.

I got this song orally from the son of the one who made it, along with
many other good songs he composed when he came to this country
sixty years ago from the Isle of Raasay. He was a kind, truthful man,
and, in addition to other things which were not to his liking, it seems
that English-speaking people did not have the same place in his
heart as those who spoke Gaelic. Cunnard was the landlord, and
Peters was his agent. Evidently both of them were merciless. If you
will be so good as to print this song in *Mac-Talla*, and if it pleases
you and your readers, perhaps I may get more of them. None of his
songs were written down, and I think it a pity. He was a gentle man,
highly respected. He was known as 'Bard MacLean who lived on the
bank.'

COMPLAINT ABOUT AMERICA

I am lonely here
in Murray Harbour² not knowing English;
it is not what I have been accustomed to,
for I always spoke Gaelic.

5 'S ann bhithinn fhéin 's mo nàbuidhean
A' mànran greis le chéil',
'S cha'n fhaic mi 'n seo ach gàrlaoich
'S cha tuig mi 'n cànain fhéin.

Gur diombach dhe mo chàirdean mi
10 Na thàinig romham fhéin,
Nach d'innis cor an àite dhomh
'S mar shàraich e iad fhéin.
A' dol troimh choill' an fhàsaich seo
Gun chàil ach rathad *blaze*;
15 O, 's muladach an t-àite seo
A' tàmh aig fear leis fhéin.

'S e th'ann a sin cùis smaointean
Mar a smaoinicheas sibh fhéin,
Cion caisbheart agus aodach
20 Air gach aon a bhios 'nam feum.
'S gun dad aig fear ri fhaotainn
Ach le 'shaothair as a' ghéig;
O, 's cianail fad an fhaoillich
Leth a shaoghal ann gu ré.

25 Cha chuir mi fios gu bràth
A dh'iarraidh chàirdean no luchd-dàimh
A thigh'nn gu ruig an àite seo
Gun talladh ach mi fhéin.
...
30 ...
Cha tigeadh sibh a thàmhachd ann
Ma tha sibh aig ur céill.

'S nam b' aithne dhomh a sgrìobhadh
Chòir 's gu'n innsinn dhuibh mo sgeul,
35 Gu'm fòghnadh leam an fhìrinn
Gus a dhéiteadh, 's nach bu bhreug.
Ged dheanadh fear a dhìchioll ann
'S an t-sìde a bhi 'ga réir,

121 A MacLean Bard from Raasay

My neighbours and I   5
used to chat at length together;
here I see only scoundrels,
and I do not understand their language.

I am offended at my relatives
who came before me;   10
they did not tell me about this place
and how it has tried them.
Going through the wilderness
there is nothing but a blazed trail;
this is truly a lonesome place   15
for one who lives by himself.

A matter of grave concern,
as you may surmise,
is the want of footwear and clothing
for each one who needs them.   20
No one can procure anything
unless he wrests it from the forest.
The length of winter is depressing;
it is fully half one's lifetime.

I'll never send word   25
to ask friends or relatives
to come to this place
with no other resident but myself.
...
...   30
You will not come to live here
if you are in your right mind.

If I knew how to write
so that I could tell my story,
the truth would suffice   35
to condemn the place; one need not dissemble.
Though one might do one's best here
when the weather is favourable,

Cùis eagail fuachd an fhaoillich ann
40 Oir reòthaidh daoine 's spréidh.

'S mór gu'm b'fheàrr bhi 'n Alba
Ged as fearainn gharbh iad fhéin;
A h-uile taobh dha'm falbhainn
Ri cois na fairge réidh.
45 Shiùbhlainn greis dhe 'n anmoch ann
'S dh'fhalbhainn 's mi leam fhéin,
Gun eagal orm gu marbhte mi
Le garbh-bhiasd dhubh nan geug.

'S ged thigeadh latha duathair oirnn
50 Le ceò 's gaoth tuath 's gun ghréin,
Cha b'ann an coille shuaimpaichean
A ghluaiseamaid ar ceum;
Ach biolair agus fuaranan
'Us luachair ghorm an t-sléibh;
55 O, b' ait' leam bhi 'n uair sin ann
A'buachailleachd na spréidh.

B'e sin an t-àite bòidheach
Gheibhte neòinean ann dha'n spréidh;
Bhiodh drùchd air bhàrr an fheòir ann
60 A' toirt fàs do'n phòr 's a' Chéit.
Bhiodh cuthagan 'us smeòraichean
A' còmhradh air bharr gheug;
'S chan fhaic mi ri mo bheò an seo
Na seòrsachan sin fhéin.

65 Dh'fhalbh sinn as an àite sin
Gu'n d'ràinig sinn seo fhéin;
An dùil gu'm faighte fàbhar ann
'S nach biodh am màl cho treun.
'S tha *Peters* 'gar sàrachdh
70 'S mur tig am bàs air fhéin,
O, 's fheudar dhuinn gu'm fàg sinn seo
'S *Cunnard* a tha 'na bhéist.

the winter cold is fearsome;
men and beasts freeze [to death].   40

Far better to be in Scotland
even though lands there be rugged, too,
no matter which direction I went
along the calm sea.
I would roam a while in the dusk there,   45
and go about alone
without fear of being killed
by wild beasts in the forests.

Even when it was a dark day,
misty, the wind from the north, and no sun in sight, 50
it was not in swampy woods
that we took a stroll,
but by water-cresses and springs
and the blue rushes on the mountain slope.
It was fun for me to be there then   55
herding the cattle.

What a beautiful place it was,
with pasture for the herd;
there was dew on the grass
quickening the seed in May.   60
The cuckoo and the mavis
harmonized in the treetops;
here I'll never see
even these again.

We left there   65
and came out here
thinking we would receive consideration,
and that the rent would not be so exacting.
But Peters is oppressing us,
and, if he doesn't die,   70
we must leave this place
and Cunnard, himself a beast.

O, 's Peters, 's truagh nach caochladh e
'S gu'n dreadh e smaoin do'n eug;
75 'S mur a seall an t-aon-fhear air
Bidh obair daor dha fhéin,
A'spurdgeadh nan daoine bochd
'S a cuir nam maor 'nan déidh.
Och, gheibh e fhathast dìoladh
80 Far nach fhaod a chuir an géill.

Iain Sinclair
(1811-1885)

Iain Sinclair represents a type of emigrant bard quite different
from Calum Bàn MacMhannain and MacLean of Murray Harbour.[1] Sinclair was born in Glendaruel, Argyllshire. He received
some education and taught school for a number of years before
he emigrated in 1840 with his widowed mother and other members of the family. The previous year he had witnessed the
departure from the glen of his cousin, Duncan Crawford, who
set out for the Clyde to board a vessel bound for Australia. The
occasion inspired one of the most popular songs directed to
specific emigrants, Sinclair's *Slàn le beanntan an fhraoich* (*Farewell
to the heather-covered bens*).[2]
Having settled in Prince Edward Island, the bard continued to

MOLADH AGUS SORAIDH CHOMHAIL

Mo shoraidh-sa gu Còmhail
Tìr bhòidheach nan lusanan,
Nan seamair 'us nan neònain,
Nan ròs 'us nan sùbhagan,
5 Nan coilltean maiseach, ceòlmhor

A pity Peters wouldn't change
and give some thought to [his] death;
if the good one doesn't have mercy on him   75
his deeds will cost him dearly,
oppressing the poor
and sending the constables after them.
He will ultimately receive retribution
where he will not be able to use it.[3]   80

---

teach for another twenty years. He remained interested in his
kinsmen of Cowal, and it was principally as a tribute to them
that he composed *Moladh agus Soraidh Chòmhail* (*Praise and Greeting to Cowal*), which he sent to the Cowal Society of Glasgow in
the early spring of 1874.[3] Although composed for a special occasion and a literate audience, the song is not unlike other emigrant songs. The bard reminisces about his scenic homeland and
its worthy heroes. He complains about the circumstances which
forced him to leave it; the glens were covered with sheep;
retainers were turned out of their dwellings; rents, tribute, and
adversity, inflicted by heartless landlords, forced the tenantry
out of the country. Consequently he favoured emigration and
the colonization of new and bountiful lands.

PRAISE AND GREETING TO COWAL

My greeting to Cowal,
the fair land of flowers,
clover and daisies,
of roses and berries
of fine forests, melodious   5

Le smeòraichean luinneagach,
Nam machraichean 's nam mór-bheann,
Nam fròg 'us nan sruthan glan.
Air fail il ithil o ro,
10 Is ho-rin-o, seinnidh mi;
Air fail il ithil o ro,
Is ho-rin-o, seinnidh mi,
Gu slàinte Comunn Chòmhail,
Na seòid chridheil, eireachdail,
15 A chumadh suas a' Ghàidhlig,
'S nach fàgadh air deireadh i.

Is i sin tìr a' chaoimhneis,
An aoibhneis, 's an t-sùbhachais,
An oilein, 's an eòlais,
20 'S nan seòid a tha curanta,
'Us cumachdail, deas, òrdail,
Bho 'm bròig suas gu 'm mullaichean;
'S iad deas-chainnteach gun bhòilich,
'S seòlta gun chluipeireachd.

25 Cha leig mi chaoidh air dì-chuimhn'
An tìm bha mi maille riu;
'S och, 's och, mo léireadh,
'S e dh'éignich thigh'nn thairis mi,
Bhi faicinn nach robh stàth dhomh
30 Bhi tàmh bheag na b'fhaid' an sin,
'S na glinn 'gan cur fo chaoraich,
'S na laoich as an dachaidhean.

Na fineachan dha'n dualchas
Bhi uasal agus eireachdail
35 Agus dìleas dha'n cinn-fheadhna
'S dha'n rìgh 's do'n eaglais ac',
'Gam fògradh as an rìoghachd
Le màl, cìs, 's eascairdeas
Nan uachdaran mhi-thruacanta,
40 Chruaidh-chridheach, bhleidireach.

with the harmonies of the mavis;
land of machairs and mountains,
of dells and clean streams.
   Air fail il ithil or ro
   is ho-rin-o, I will sing   10
   Air fail il ithil o ro,
   Is ho-rin-o, I will sing
to the health of the Cowal Society,
the courageous, noble men,
who would keep up the Gaelic   15
and not forsake it.

It is the land of kindness
of cheer and happiness,
of the scholar and learning,
of heroes who are bold,   20
stately, well-groomed, neat,
from head to foot,
eloquent without ostentation,
cunning without deceit.

I shall never forget   25
the time I spent among them.
But, alas, my ruin,
what necessitated my coming out
was seeing that there was no advantage
in my staying there much longer,   30
since the glens were being filled with sheep
and the folk driven from their homes.

The clans, who by heredity
were noble and splendid,
true to their chief,   35
to their king and their church,
are now being exiled from their kingdom
by rents, taxes, and the hostility
of the merciless landlords,
hard-hearted, importunate men.   40

Ged 's deacair seo 'nar sùil-ne
Bha a' chùis air a suidheachadh;
Oir 's iomchuidh gu'm bi dùthchannan
Ur air an tuineachadh.
45 'S gun Bhreatunnaich a shàrach'
Chan fhàg iad an t-eilean ac',
Ged 's mór a b'fheàrr do phàirt dhiubh
Bhith tàmh an America.

Ma 's e 's gu'm bi iad grìdeil
50 'Us dìchiollach, oidhirpeach,
Gun mi-fhortan bhith 'n dàn dhaibh,
Ach slàn, làidir, adhartach,
Mu'm bi iad fad' 's an tìr seo,
Cho cinnteach 's tha coill' innte,
55 Bidh aca crodh 'us caoraich,
Biadh, aodach, 's mór ghoireasan.

Ged a tha 'n geamhradh cruaidh,
Reòta, fuar, sneachdach, gaillionnach,
Bidh aca taighean blàth,
60 'S teine làidir a gharas iad.
'S cha bhi cùram fuachd daibh,
'S coille bhuan ri gearradh ac'.
Ma thig sibh nall à Còmh'll,
Tha mi'n dòchas nach aithreach leibh.

Although baffling to our eyes,
events had already been predestined;
it must needs be that new lands
be colonized.
Unless Britons are oppressed,   45
they will not leave their island,
though it would be much better for some of them
to live in America.

If they are hardy,
diligent, persevering,   50
with no mischance in store for them,
and if they are healthy, strong, progressive,
before long in this country,
as sure as there is a forest here,
they will have sheep and cattle,   55
food, clothing, and abundant comforts.

Although winter is hard,
frosty, cold, snowy, stormy,
they will have warm houses
and a roaring fire to warm them.   60
They will not fear the cold,
for they will have an inexhaustible forest to cut.
If you come here from Cowal
I am confident that you will have no regrets.

4 Ontario

Anna Gillis
(dates unknown)

When the *MacDonald* sailed from Greenock to Quebec in the fall of 1786, Anna Gillis of Morar was one of the five hundred emigrants on board.[1] The entire group was destined for Upper Canada where many of their kinsmen had already settled in Glengarry county, following the American Revolution.[2] It seems likely that Anna Gillis and her husband, a MacDonald from Knoydart, settled close to the township of Charlottenburg, possibly in Roxburgh or Finch, in what is now Stormont county.[3]

Traditions current in Cape Breton about fifty years ago seem to be the only direct evidence about this bard and her songs.[4] It was thought there that she had lived briefly in eastern Nova Scotia at some time; it was also thought that she was the grandmother of John Sandfield MacDonald, first premier of Ontario. Numerous inquiries have failed to elicit supporting evidence for these views. It is known that John Sandfield's parents emigrated from Scotland in 1786, and his birthdate is given as 1812.[5] Thus it is not altogether improbable that one of his parents was of the Gillis-MacDonald family. In 1879 Alexander MacKenzie, editor of the *Celtic Magazine*, visited North America and recorded his visit in some detail. He described the Sandfield MacDonalds as Gaelic-speaking descendants of Knoydart emigrants, with specific reference to Honourable Donald Alex, lieutenant-governor of Ontario, whose father lived on a farm at Sandfield Corner near St Raphael's church.[6] It could be that the Cape Breton tradition confused the two distinguished political figures. In any event, such a supposition sheds no further light, for the present, on their possible connection with Anna Gillis.

Before Anna Gillis left Morar, she composed one of the two known songs ascribed to her, *O, siud an taobh a ghabhainn* (*That is the road I would take*).[7] It is a descriptive song, touching lightly but affectionately on the rugged contours of the homeland, the great Clan Donald with their ancient arms, the sounds and songs on the mountain and in the forests of the Gàidhealtachd. The

---

O, SIUD AN TAOBH A GHABHAINN

Gabhaidh sinn ar cead de Mhòrair,
Arasaig 's Mùideart na mòr-bheann,
Eige 's Canaidh gheal nan ròiseal,
'S Uibhist bhòidheach ghreannmhor.
5   O, siud an taobh a ghabhainn,
E, siud an taobh a ghabhainn,
'S gach aon taobh am biodh an rathad,
Ghabhainn e gu h-eòlach.

Cnòideart fuar 'us Gleann a Garaidh
10   Far am bheil na fiùrain gheala,
'S Uisge Ruadh o'n Bhràighe thairis
Gu Srath Inbhir Lòchaidh.

Tha na càirdean gasda, lìonmhor,
Thall 's a bhos air feadh nan crìochan;
15   'S ma dh'fhàgas mi h-aon dhiubh 'n dìochuimhn'
'S aobhar mìothlachd dhòmhs' e.

Dòmhnullaich 'us gu'm bu dual dhaibh
Seasamh dìreach ri achd cruadail,

shadow of emigration falls on all of these, but the song concludes with a note of optimism as the author looks to freedom and prosperity across the sea.

It would seem that Anna's expectations were not fulfilled at first. She found pioneer life difficult and lonely. Father Alexander (Scotus) MacDonell, the leader and pastor who had accompanied the Knoydart emigrants to Glengarry in 1786, urged her to accept her lot cheerfully. She responded to his counsel with the song *Canada Ard* (*Upper Canada*), a neat, favourable commentary on the good fortune of those who had been led from bondage by their solicitous Maighstir Alasdair.[8]

THAT IS THE ROAD I WOULD TAKE

We'll take leave of Morar,
Arisaig, and mountainous Moidart,
Eigg, and fair, surf-swept Canna,
and beautiful, lovely Uist.
    That is the road I would take;   5
    that is the road I would take;
    and wherever the road lay
    I would take it for I know it well.

Knoydart and Glengarry,
where there are white saplings,   10
and the Red Stream from the Brae
over to the glen of Inverlochy.

Gallant, numerous are the kinsmen,
here and there throughout these areas;
if I forget any of them   15
it will be a cause of deep regret to me.

The MacDonalds were always wont
to stand boldly in the face of hardship,

A bhith diann a'ruith na ruaige,
20 Dìleas, cruaidh gu dòruinn.

Long 's leòmhann, craobh 'us caisteal,
Bhiodh 'nan sròiltean àrd ri 'm faicinn;
Fìreun, 'us làmh dhearg 'us bradan,
'Us fraoch 'na bhadain còmh' riuth'.

25 Chì mi 'n cabrach air an fhuaran,
A ghréidh fhéin 'nan treud mu'n cuairt dha.
A h-uile té 's a sròn 's an fhuaradh
Mu'n tig gnùis luchd-tòrachd.

Leam bu bhinn a' chaismeachd mhaidne,
30 An déidh dùsgadh as mo chadal,
Coileach dubh air bhàrr a' mheangain,
'S fiadh 's a' bhad ri crònan.

Falbhaidh sinn o thìr nan uachdran;
Ruigidh sinn an dùthaich shuaimhneach,
35 Far am bidh crodh laoigh air bhuailtean,
Air na fuarain bhòidheach.

Falbhaidh sinn, 's cha dean sinn fuireach;
Fàgaidh sinn slàn agaibh uile.
Seòlaidh sinn air bhàrr na tuinne;
40 Dia chur turus òirnne.

CANADA ARD

Ann an Canada Ard
Tha gach sonas 'us àgh;
Bidh gach maoin ann a' fàs ri chéile.

Gu bheil cruithneachd a' fàs,
5 Luchdmhor, lìonte gu' bhàrr,
Ach trì mìosan thoirt dha de thearmunn.

eagerly putting opponents to rout,
faithful, intrepid in adversity.   20

Ship and lion, tree and castle,
visible on their raised standards,
the eagle, the red hand, the salmon,
the sprigs of heather.[9]

I see the stag at the spring,   25
his herd like warriors around him;
each one with its nose in the wind
lest a huntsman appear.

Sweet to me was the morning music
when I awoke from sleep;   30
a black cock in the treetops
and the deer bellowing in the thickets.

We shall leave the land of the lairds;
we'll go to the land of contentment,
where there will be cattle in the folds   35
and around the fine pools.

We shall leave and not delay;
we'll bid you all farewell.
We'll sail over the billows.
God speed us.   40

UPPER CANADA

In Upper Canada
there is every joy and delight;
all requirements will prosper together.

Wheat grows
abundantly, ready to harvest,   5
with only three months to bring it to full season.

Gheibhear siùcar à craobh
Ach an goc chur 'na taobh,
'Us cha dochair sin a h-aon de geugan.

10   Gheibh sinn mil agus fìon,
'S gach ni eile gu'r miann;
Cha bhi uireasbhuidh sìon fo'n ghréin oirnn.

Maighstir Alasdair òg,
Mac Fear Scotais na sròil,
15   Sagart beannaicht' bha mór le éibhneas.

Dh'fhalbh e leinne mar naomh
Gus ar beatha bhi saor,
Mar dh'fhalbh iad le Maois o'n Eipheit.

Fhuair sinn bailtean dhuinn fhìn,
20   Le còir dhainginn o'n rìgh,
'S cha bhi uachdrain a chaoidh 'gar léireadh.

An Anonymous Glengarry Bard
(dates unknown)

One of the most unusual of emigrant songs, *Tha mise fo ghruai-mean* (*I am melancholy*), was recorded from Donald Fletcher, a ninety-three year old informant, residing in 1960 in Dunvegan, Glengarry County, Ontario.[1] The circumstances which gave rise to the song were also related by Fletcher in a delightful Gaelic introduction, of which the following is a transcription:

Tha seann òran ann a' seo, agus 's e duine Gàidheal bho'n t-seann
dùthaich a thàinig a nall, agus cha robh e eòlach air an dùthaich,
's cha robh an dùthaich eòlach air. Agus tha cuileagan uaine 's an
dùthaich seo. 'S iad cuileagan uaine 's a latha ann agus 's an
oidhche 'fàs 'nan teine. Chaidh an duine seo air falbh a dh'àite
comharsanach, 's bha e tigh'nn dhachaidh. Bha 'n oidhche dorcha.

Sugar may be gotten from a tree
if a tap be inserted in its side,
and not one of its branches damaged.

We shall have berries and wine   10
and all else that we desire;
we shall lack nothing under the sun.

Young Father Alexander,
son of Scotus of the banners,
the holy priest, was full of kindness.   15

Like a saint he brought us out
so that we would be free
as were those who followed Moses out of Egypt.

We got farms of our own
with proprietory rights from the king,[10]   20
and landlords will no more oppress us.

Thoisich na cuileagan uaine air fàs 'nan teine 'us bha iad 'dol mu'n
cuairt dhà 'ga leantainn, 's e 'n dùil gu robh iad a' dol a chur teine
ris, 's rinn e 'n t-òran seo. Gabhaidh me ceathramh no dhà dheth.

This is an old song, and it was a Highlander from the old country
who came over, and he didn't know the country and the country
didn't know him. There are green flies in this country. They are
green in the daytime, and at night they turn into fire. This man went
to visit a neighbour, and he was coming home. The night was dark.
The flies began to turn into fire, and they were around him, following him, and he thought they were going to set him on fire. Then he
made this song. I'll sing a verse or two of it.

Probably *Tha mise fo ghruaimean* was much longer than what remains of it today, but happily for those who are interested in the literary efforts of Highland emigrants, the following verses

---

THA MISE FO GHRUAIMEAN

O, tha mise fo ghruaimean,
'S beag ioghnadh ged a ghluaisinn duilich;
'S fad' tha mi bho I mo chàirdean
Far 'n d' rinn mi a fàgail uile.
5   O, tha mise fo ghruaimean.

'S iomadh rud a tha 's an àit' seo
Nach robh 's an àit' a dh'fhàg sinne;
Cuileagan uaine 's an là ann,
'S air an oidhch' a' fàs 'nan teine.
10 O, tha mise fo ghruaimean.

'S ged is liath ceann an dròbhair
Thàinig nall còmhla ruinne,
Bha na suaimpeachain cho dlùth ann
'S gu'n dh'éibh e, 'Tha 'n dùthaich 'na teine.'
15 O, tha mise fo ghruaimean.

Cha chluinn sibh cuthag no gug-gùg ann,
Maduinn chiùin air bràigh glinne;
Ach drumaireachd nan coilich-ruadha,
'S siud a' fuaim tha fuathach dhuinne.
20 O, tha mise fo ghruaimean.

have been recovered. It may be too late to look for specific information about the author, who, as indicated in the song, was a
native of Iona.

I AM MELANCHOLY

I am melancholy;
little wonder that I go about sad,
for I am far from Iona, land of my kindred,
where I left them all.
I am melancholy.   5

There are many things here
which were not in the land we left;
green flies in the daytime
which turn into fire at night.
I am melancholy.   10

Though grey the head of the Drover[2]
who emigrated with us,
the swamps were so dense
that he called out, 'The land is on fire.'
I am melancholy.   15

You'll not hear the cuckoo nor his 'coo-coo' here
on a fine morning in the upper glen,
but only the drumming of the red cock,
and that sound is unpleasant to us.
I am melancholy.   20

Hugh MacCorkindale / Eobhan Mac-Corcadail
(dates unknown)

All that is known about this bard is what can be inferred from one of his songs, *Oran le seann Ileach* (*Song of an old Islayman*), sent to *An Gàidheal* in 1877 for publication.[1] He was then living in Sullivan, Ontario, having left Islay over twenty years before. When MacCorkindale was a young man, his landlord had been a gentle master, kind and considerate towards his tenants. Through some mischance the benign laird lost his holdings, and subsequently the region was deserted, save for the ubiquitous sheep. Emigration took its toll there as elsewhere in the Highlands.

MacCorkindale remembered his homeland with considerable rancour, but found it possible to make a good living in Ontario. The exact circumstances of his coming are obscure. The *Directory* for the township of Sullivan in Grey county, 1886-7, lists three

ORAN LE SEANN ILEACH

Tha còrr 'us fichead bliadhna thìm
Bho'n dh'fhàg mi glinn mo dhùthchais;
Bu nì gun fheum bhi fuireach ann,
Bha cosnadh gann 's an dùthaich.
5 Thug mi sgrìob gu tìr nan Gall
'S mi 'n geall air beagan cùinnidh;
Cha do chòrd iad idir rium
'Us cha robh càil 's na cùisean.

Idir cha robh càil dhomh fhéin
10 'Us dh'fhàg mi 'm dhéidh na Bùrgaich;
'S a Chanada a nall gu'n d'thàinig,
Aite b'fheàrr dhomh dùbailt.

MacCorkindales: Alan at Keady, and John and Hugh at Marmion.[2] The last named may have been the poet. It is difficult to determine if there was a second Gaelic poet in Sullivan in that decade. The song *Comhairle do no Gàidheil a tha 'fuireach an Albainn* (*Advice to Highlanders living in Scotland*), also ascribed to Hugh MacCorkindale, was sent from there to *An Gàidheal* in 1871.

The MacCorkindales had a long bardic tradition. A poem in the *Book of the Dean of Lismore*[3] is ascribed to Aith Bhreac Inghean Coirceadail, probably the wife of the chief of the Clan MacNeil, who was constable of Castle Sween in Knapdale for the Lord of the Isles about 1455. *Oran le Seann Ileach* is far removed from its roots in time and space. Nonetheless, it does represent the continuity of tradition which has characterized countless Gaelic communities overseas for almost two centuries.

SONG OF AN ISLAYMAN

It is now more than twenty years
since I left my ancestral glens;
it was useless to remain there
for employment was scarce in the land.
I took a trip to the Lowlands   5
where I had promise of small earnings;
I didn't like things at all,
and prospects were not attractive.

They did not appeal to me at all,
and I left the townspeople behind.   10
Then I came over to Canada,
a place twice as good for me.

'Us fhuair mi cosnadh ann gun tàir,
'S mo phàidheadh cha bu diù e;
15 'Us bho sin gu ruig an t-àm seo
Cha robh fang mu m' chùrsa.

Tha cùrsa dhaoine math gu leòir
Le dachaidh bhòidheach, fhaoilidh;
Nì nach fhaiceadh iad ri 'm beò,
20 Le còmhnachadh an taobh sin.
B'e là an àigh do mhóran Ghàidheal
Sheòl thair sàile 'n taobh seo
Le 'n cuid ghearran ann am pàircean,
Crodh, 'us bàrr, 'us caoraich.

25 Tha taighean-cloich 'us taighean-*brige*
frame 'us *log* aig tuathnaich;
'S a'chuid as mò' dhiubh siud le orsaid
Dosarrach ri 'n guailnean.
Na craobhan lùbte làn de dh'ùbhlan,
30 Torrach, sùghail, uaine;
Plums 's peuran, *grapes* 'us caorainn,
Smiaran 's dearcan-ruadha.

Tha 'n tìr seo math do 'n duine bhochd,
'S do 'n bheairteach mar an ceudna;
35 Gach aon dhiubh dol a réir a neart,
An ghìomh, an teach, 's an éideadh;
Ach daoine leisg 'us luchd na misg,
Tha ghoirt gu tric 'gan léireadh;
'S an duine ionraic gheibh e meas,
40 Bidh aige stòc 'us feudail.

Tha reòthadh mor 'us sneachda trom'
Air uachdar gruinnd 's a' gheamhradh;
Ach tha na h-aodaichean d'an réir,
Gu 'r dìon bho bheum na gailbhinn.
45 'Us tha ar n-eich le 'n cruidhean geur
A' tarrainn *sleigh* gu meanmach;

I was employed there without discrimination,
and my pay was not the worst;
from that day to this   15
there was no obstacle to my progress.

Here men fare well enough,
with fine, prosperous homes,
something they would not see in their lifetime
had they remained on the other side.   20
It was a lucky day for many Highlanders
when they sailed over here;
[now they have] geldings in their fields,
cattle, crops, and sheep.

The settlers have stone houses, brick houses,   25
frame and log houses;
most of these have an orchard
well branched up to their eaves.
Trees bend over, laden with apples,
bulging, succulent, green.   30
There are plums, pears, grapes, rowan-berries,
blackberries, bilberries.

This country is good for the poor man
and for the rich man as well.
Each one lives according to his means,   35
[reflected] in his pursuits, his home, and his clothing.
But lazy people and drunkards
are often afflicted with poverty;
the upright man is respected,
[for] he has stock and wealth.   40

Heavy frost and deep snow
cover the ground in winter,
but suitable clothing
protects us from the bitterness of the storms.
Our sharp shod horses   45
draw the sleighs swiftly;

A mach 'us dhachaidh thig gun éis,
'S dh'fhàg iad lòd nan déidh rinn airgiod.

An uair a' siud mi leis an tuaigh
50 A thoirt a nuas nan craobhan,
Bha 'n obair trom, ach dh'éireadh sunnd
'N uair chìteadh ceann dhiubh 'g aomadh,
A' deanamh turran fada cruinn
'S an loinn a bh'fheàrr a shaoilinn;
55 A ghabhadh losgadh ann an àm,
'S bha cruineachd trom 'na dhéidh sin.

Bidh na stocan gu bhi loisgte
Ann a sia no seachd de bhliadhnan;
'S tha na pàircean fada, réidh,
60 'S an spréidh 'nam measg ag ionaltradh.
Agus seo 'na fhearann saor
Aig daoine fhuair am pianadh
Anns an tìr a dh'fhàg nan déidh
'S a bha 'nan éiginn riamh ann.

65 Tha iad saor bho mhaor na bàirlinn,
'S bho àrdan an uachdarain;
Bho gach *factor* agus bàillidh
B'àbhaist bhi 'gan gualadh,
'S a' toirt a nuas an còmhdaich chinn
70 Ged reòthadh lom a' ghruag dhiubh.
'S cha dean mòrlanachd no tàir
Gu bràth an cuir fo ghruaimean.

Bheir mi nis anns a' chomh-dhùnadh
Cliù do rìgh nan àirdean,
75 A dh'fhosgail dhuinne dùthaich ùr
'Us cùisean tha gu 'r fàbhar.
Faodaidh daoine cur 'us buain
Gun uamhas romh na màil orr',
'S do'n duine bhochd chan 'eil fo'n ghréin
80 'Ga fheum an tìr is fheàrr dha.

going forth and returning home without delay
leaving behind a load worth money.

When I set out with my axe
to fell the trees   50
the work was hard, but it was heartening
to see their tops bending,
then causing a tremor all around,
falling in the direction I thought best.
They could be burnt in due time,   55
and a heavy crop of wheat would then grow in their place.

The stumps can be burnt out
in six or seven years;
the fields are broad and level,
with cattle grazing in them.   60
This is a free land
for people who suffered extortion
in the country they left,
where they were always in need.

They are free from the summons of agents   65
and from the landlord's arrogance;
from every factor and bailie
who used to harass them
and bring the roof down over their heads
even though their hair might freeze off.   70
Neither servile labour nor contempt
will ever dishearten them [here].

Now in conclusion I will render
honour to the God above,
who opened up for us a new country   75
and circumstances favourable to us.
People may sow and reap
without dread of rents,
and for the poor man there is not under the sun
a land better suited to his needs.   80

'S an Eilein Ileach bha mi òg,
Duin' uasal còir b'e 'n t-uachdaran;
Bha e math do'n duine bhochd,
'S cha d'rinn e lochd air tuath'nach.
85 Ach chaill e 'n t-àite, ni bha cràiteach,
Rinn seo nàisnich fhuadach;
Tha gach taigh 'us baile fàs
'S tha caoraich 'n àite 'n t-sluaigh ann.

Ach ma thig orra gu h-obunn
90 Cogadh thar na cuaintean,
'S beag a ni na caoraich mhaol
Le gunna caol 's an uair sin.
Cha bhi Gàidheal dol gu blàr
A chumas nàmhaid bhuapa;
95 Is beag an dolaidh, rinn iad tàir
Air Clann mo ghràidh 'gam fuadach.

When I was young in Islay
the landlord was a noble, gentle man;
he was good to the poor man,
and did no harm to his tenantry.
But he lost his estate, a disastrous matter,   85
which caused the natives to be evicted;
every house, every farm is vacant,
and sheep have replaced people there.

If suddenly war should come upon them
from across the seas,   90
polled sheep can do little
in the face of guns at such a time.
No Gaels will go to war
to protect them from their enemies.
Small is the pity; they rejected   95
my beloved clansmen, sending them into exile.

5 Manitoba and the Northwest Territories

Dòmhnall Diombach (Resentful Donald) and
his Compatriot (dates unknown)

Bards like Dòmhnall Diombach and his compatriot were numbered among the hardy band of Highlanders whose role in
opening up the Canadian West is in itself epical. Little is known
about these two bards, if indeed there were two. It is possible
that both songs edited here are the work of the same man, adapt-
ing the tradition of flyting (poetry of mutual abuse), a form of
composition well known among Scottish bards.

A description of the pioneer settlers of St Andrew's, Saskatchewan, indicates that pipers, seanaichies, and bards brought
music and merriment to that part of the great west towards the
end of the nineteenth century.[1] At least one woman and two
men were reputed to have some bardic ability. The most notable
of these was Donald MacKinnon (Dòmhnall Og or Young
Donald) of Balivanich, Benbecula, who 'composed many pieces
of merit, some of which are vivid pictures of the ups and downs
of pioneer life in the early days.'[2] *Teist Dhòmhnaill air Manitóba*
(*Donald's Testimony about Manitoba*) is one such vivid picture and
may be ascribed tentatively to this bard.[3]

Dòmhnall Diombach's references to Sir George Stephen suggest that he had procured his land grant from the Canadian
Pacific Railway, of which Sir George was president. In 1882 Sir
James Rankin invested $160,000 in a colonizing venture at Elk-
horn, Manitoba. He devised a scheme of grants by which each
settler was obliged to render him one-half of his annual crop.
Rankin's enterprise ended in bankruptcy, but the fifty per cent

proviso of his scheme was adopted successfully by the CPR.[4] That proviso was one of several aspects of prairie pioneering which caused the resentful bard to look covetously to Dakota.

So serious was the fury of emigration from Manitoba to Dakota between 1874 and 1882 that Canadian agents were commissioned to investigate the causes of the exodus.[5] Dakota had become 'Runaway Harbour' for thousands of settlers from Que-

---

TEIST DHOMHNAILL AIR MANITOBA

'S mór an sluagh a dh'fhàg na Bàigh
Gu tighinn gu Manitóba chrainndidh;
Nam b'e 'n diugh an dé do phàirt dhinn
Gum biodh dàil 'nar seòladh.

5   Dh'fhàg sinn dùthaich fhallain bhlàth
Bha tàcharach an taic an t-sàile,
Ged bha na h-uachdaran 'nam plàigh,
Bha sinn air làr ar n-eòlais.

Chaidh sinn gu h-uachdaran charach
10 A reic sinn coluinn agus anam
Ri rathad-iaruinn gun bheannachd
'S feannar sinn gu'r brògan.

Fhuair triùcairean an dùthaich rapach
Air sia sgillinn an t-acair;
15 Aig dà dholar chruinn is cairteal,
Ni am prasgan stòras.

Rinneadh plot de dhroch-bheart suas
Air taobh bhos is thall a'chuain
Chum gum mealladh iad an sluagh
20 Gu tìr an fhuachd 's an dòlais.

Tha coileach-feucaig an Dun-éideann
Leis nach truagh an tuath 'nan éiginn;

bec as well as from the west. Dòmhnall Diombach was tempted
to join them. His compatriot tried to dissuade him. It is to be
hoped that he succeeded, for the Dakota dream was short-lived.
Depression and poverty swept the area in the middle eighties,
and both the rich land and the gold which attracted Manitoba
residents were then as accessible on their own alkali holdings as
they were across the border.

DONALD'S TESTIMONY ABOUT MANITOBA

Great was the host who left the Bays[6]
to come to windswept Manitoba;
if today were yesterday for some of us
we would have been reluctant to sail.

We left a healthy, warm land   5
of plenty by the sea.
Although the overlords were a plague
We were on familiar terrain.

We went to her wily overlords,   10
who sold us body and soul
to the railroad, the unblessed,
and we are being skinned to our shoes.

The rogues acquired the wretched land
for six shillings an acre;
at a round two and a quarter   15
the villains will make a fortune.

A vicious plot was devised
on both sides of the ocean
in order to lure people
to this cold and forbidding land.   20

There is a peacock in Edinburgh[7]
who has no sympathy for those in need;

Nan iarradh Emily ar ceusadh
Bhiodh an t-eun ud deònach.

25 Bha mìle breugair airson duais
Le leabhraichean a' dol mun cuairt,
A' moladh na h-àirde 'n iar-thuath
'S gach buaidh bh'air Manitóba.

Cha robh beachd-sgeòil bu deòin le cailleach
30 Bho Bhun-Leòdhais gu Ceann Bharraidh
Nach deach a leughadh mu'n fhearann
Le geallanna gun sòradh.

Ràinig sinn 'Fearann a' Gheallaidh,'
Bha'n reòthadh cho cruaidh ri stallaidh,
35 Còrr is dà throigh dheug 'san talamh,
Cha bhiodh seangan beò ann.

Dh'fhoighneachd mi de Dhòmhnall Chaluim
'Cuin thig an deigh as an talamh?'
Thuirt e le tùirse rium, 'A charaid,
40 Fanaidh i ri d'bheò ann.'

B'fheàrr leam na a' bhó-laoigh a b'fheàrr
Bha riamh aig bodaich Inbhir-Air,
Nach do chreid mi bhreug bho'n ghràisg
Mu fhàsach Mhanitóba.

45 'S iomadh allaban a's cuaradh
Aig daoine anns an tìr gun tuar,
Bidh gaoth a tuath le nuallan fuar
A' toirt nan cluas 's nan sròin dhinn.

'Nar fàrdaich gun tuar am fuar-mhaduinn,
50 Bidh liath-reòthadh air a' phlaide,
Bùrn agus liunn, meug no bainne
Mar ghlainneachan reòite.

Nuair bhios *blizzard* 'san tìr aognaidh,
Feumar béin gach béist mar aodach,

if Emily[8] should request our crucifixion
that vulture would accede to it.

A thousand liars, well rewarded,   25
went about with books
extolling the North West
and the excellence of Manitoba.

There was no information pleasing to women,
from the Butt of Lewis to Barra Head,   30
that was not being propagated about the land,
with unhesitating promises.

We reached the land of promise,
The frost was as hard as rock,
more than twelve feet into the ground;   35
not even an ant could survive it.

I asked Donald Malcolm,[9]
'When will the ice leave the ground?'
He replied ruefully, 'Friend,
it will remain there a lifetime.'   40

I would prefer to the best herd
which the men of Inverary ever had,
that I had not believed the lies of the mob
concerning the wilds of Manitoba.

Much fatigue and agony   45
the people endure in this hopeless land.
The north wind with its moaning blast
whips off our ears and noses.

In our cheerless houses in the cold morning
there is hoarfrost on the blankets;   50
water and ale, whey or milk,
all like frozen glass.

When there is a blizzard in the bleak land
one needs the fur of every animal for clothing.

55 Cha dean clò de chlòimh ar saoradh,
    Bheir a' ghaoth an fheòil dhinn.

    An Albainn am maduinn Chéitein
    Rachainn cas-ruisgt' thun nan sléibhtean
    Cha bhiodh feum air mogais éitidh,
60   'S cha bhiodh béin 'gar còmhdach.

    'S sinn a rinn imrich gun àgh
    Gu boglaich Mhanitóba ghrànda,
    Chan iarrainn tuilleadh de dh'ànradh
    Dha m'namhaid na tha oirnne.

65 Bidh sinn ag obair mar thràillean
    Air fearann *Alcah* bàite,
    Ged a thogamaid am bàrr,
        Bidh cus de'n ghràn aig Seòras.

    Bidh trian no còrr dheth dheòin no dh'aindeòin
70 Aig rathad iaruinn airson fàraidh,
    Goill is Gàidheil air am mealladh,
        'S am fearann fo *mhortgage*.

    Tha clann nan treun-fhear gleusda maiseach,
    Bu mhath gu feum air sléibh 's air machair,
75 An diugh 'gan léireadh, 's béin 'gan seacadh,
        'S cuid d'an casan reòite.

    Mas beò mi gus an tig an t-earrach,
    Fàgaidh mi 'fearann a' Gheallaidh'
    Ruigidh mi Dakota thall ud –
80   Tha fearann agus òr ann.

FREAGRADH DO DHOMHNALL DIOMBACH

'S olc an obair do 'n a' bhàrd
Bhi cur bacail air na sàir,

Woollen tweed will not protect us;   55
the wind whips our flesh off.

In Scotland on a May morning
I would go barefooted to the moors;
there was no need of the ugly moccasin,
nor were we clothed in furs.   60

It was we who made the luckless move
to boggy, ugly Manitoba.
I wouldn't wish any greater misfortune
on my foe than what has befallen us.

We work like slaves   65
on the drenched alkali land.
Though we should raise a crop
George would have a great part of it.[10]

A third of it, like it or lump it,
will be taken by the railroad for freight;   70
Lowlanders and Gaels are being deceived,
and their lands mortgaged.

Sons of the hardy, adventurous heroes
skilful on moor and dale,
are today in great distress, chafing in their skins,   75
some with frozen feet.

If I survive until spring
I shall leave the 'Land of Promise.'
I'll go to Dakota;
land and gold abound there.   80

REPLY TO RESENTFUL DONALD

It is an evil work for the bard
to restrain the worthy men

Da 'm bu chòir a thighinn gun dàil
A thàmh do Mhanitòba.

5 'S iomadh buaidh a th'air an àit'
Rinn thu dhiomoladh 'nad dhàn;
'S gheibh thu mach an ùine gheàrr
Gu feàrr e na Dakota.

Ged tha an geamhradh reòta, fuar,
10 Cha chuir siud oirnn geilt no gruaim;
Aimsir shoilleir, thioram, chruaidh,
Cur dreach an gruaidh ar n-òigridh.

Théid sinn gu clachan 's gu féill,
Air ar còmhdach ann am béin;
15 'S cha bhi domail dhuinn no beud
Ged shéideadh a' ghaoth reòta.

'N uair a thig an t-earrach le spìd
Théid gach fear a chuir an t-sìol;
'S cha bhi mathachadh dhìth
20 Air talamh mìn a' chòmhnaird.

'N uair a thig am foghair mu'n cuairt
Théid na machraichean a bhuain;
'S cha bhi duine gun a dhuais
A' giùlan sguaban òr-bhuidh'.

25 Tìr an toraidh, tìr an àigh,
Tìr na tuirneip 's a' bhuntàt,
Tìr 's an dean an cruineachd fàs,
An coirce bàn 's an t-eòrna.

Tìr na saorsa, tìr nam buadh,
30 Far nach leagair màl air tuath,
'S far nach faicir bàillidh cruaidh
A' cur an t-sluaigh air fògradh.

who should come without delay
to live in Manitoba.

There are many fine features in the place   5
which you dispraised in your song;
and you will discover very soon
that it is better than Dakota.

Although the winter is frosty and cold,
that does not cause us fear or gloom;   10
the sunny, dry, bracing weather
animates the faces of the young.

We go to church and to festivities
well protected in furs;
no harm or injury will come to us   15
though the cold wind blows.

When spring comes quickly,
each one goes to sow seed;
fertilizer is not required
by the fine soil of the plains.   20

When autumn comes round
the fields are harvested;
no one will be without his reward,
gathering golden-yellow stooks.

Land of bounty, land of joy,   25
land of the turnip and the potato,
land where wheat grows
and white oats and barley.

Land of the free, land of endowments,
where rent is not demanded from the tenants,   30
and where the cruel bailie is not seen
forcing the people into exile.

'M fear a thig dhiubh ann an cabhaig
Gheibh e taghadh air an fhearann;
35 'S 'n uair bhios càch gun crodh, gun aighean,
Bidh esan dheth gu dòigheil.

'S iomadh Gàidheal smiorail, cruaidh,
Dh'fhàg a dhùthaich falamh, fuar,
A tha 'n diugh 'na shuidhe suas
40 Le uaislean Mhanitóba.

Ann an eaglais, 's anns an stàid,
'S leis na Gàidheil urram àrd.
'S mór an onair siud a ghnàth
Do'n tìr a dh'àraich òg iad.

45 Mo luchd-dùthcha th'ann an éis,
Fàgaibh fearann nach leibh fhéin.
Thigibh thar fairge 'nur leum,
'S na d'thugaibh géill do Dhòmhnull.

Angus MacIntosh
(dates unknown)

A distinct change in the mood and manner of Highland emigration is evident in the song *Dh'fhàg sinn cladach Alb' an dé* (*We left the shore of Scotland yesterday*), composed by Angus MacIntosh as he crossed the Atlantic at the turn of the present century.[1] This poet settled ultimately at Fort Qu'Appelle, Assiniboia, North West Territories, and from there he sent the song to the *Celtic Monthly* for publication in 1905.[2]

As indicated in an editorial note introducing the song, the voyage was safe and smooth in a modern vessel, one of the Allan Liners,[3] manned by seasoned sailors from Mull and Islay. Men danced to the piper's lively tunes; laments were no longer fitting

He who comes early
gets his choice of land;
while others lack cattle and chattels,   35
he is well established.

Many an energetic, hardy Gael,
who left his deserted, unfriendly homeland,
sits today
among the distinguished in Manitoba.   40

In church and state
the Gaels hold high rank.
That is a great tribute
to the land that reared them in their youth.

Oh my kinsmen, who are in want,   45
leave the land which does not belong to you.
Come at once across the ocean,
and pay no heed to Donald.

---

for such an occasion. Evictions and clearances were over; the
seven hundred Scots on board were leaving their country, not
through necessity, but with a spirit of high adventure. They
were preoccupied with thoughts of the broad lands and great
forests of central and western Canada. They would go their
separate ways after they arrived in Quebec, but they would
remain united in a common loyalty to the homeland. In the final
lines of the song, the poet exhorts them never to let their youth-
ful ardour for the old country diminish. With or without the
exhortation, they were not likely to do so. Prosperity in the New
World was not incompatible with the Gael's enduring allegiance
to the Old.

DH'FHAG SINN CLADACH ALB' AN DE

Dh'fhàg sinn cladach Alb' an dé
'Us gach gleann 'us beann 'us tullach,
Air am bi gu bràth ar déidh,
'S far am bheil luchd-gaoil a' fuireach.
5   Sgoltadh thonn, sgoltadh thonn,
Sgoltadh thonn cuan nan gaillionn;
Sgoltadh thonn, sgoltadh thonn,
Leis an long 's feàrr aig Ailean.

Chan eil mulad air aon ghnùis,
10 Chan eil aon sùil a' sileadh;
Tha gach neach an geall air òr,
'Us le stòr dol a thilleadh.

'Us an àite port a' bhròin –
Cumha Dhòmhnuill Bhàin MhicCruimein –
15 'S ann tha 'm pìobaire th'air bòrd
Cur na seòid dhanns' 's a mhireadh.

'Us tha 'n long gun bhréid, gun seòl
Ach le innleachdan 's teine,
Strachdadh tonnan garg le 'sròin,
20 'Us 'gan cur 'nan ceò le deireadh.

Air tìr chrannach, mhór, an iar,
Tha a sròin air a cumail,
Leis na fir nach stiùireadh clì,
Gillean Il' agus Mhuile.

25 Cluinnear aon a'seinneadh cliù
Tìr nam bàirde gun ghainne,
Air am bheil gach smuain 'us sùil,
'S air am bheil sinn dlùth a' teannadh.

WE LEFT THE SHORE OF SCOTLAND YESTERDAY

We left the shore of Scotland yesterday
and every glen and ben and knoll,
which we shall forever cherish,
where our beloved kinsmen dwell.
    Riving waves, riving waves,   5
    Riving waves on the stormy seas;
    Riving waves, riving waves,
    with the best of the Allan Liners.

There is sadness on no countenance,
not one eye weeps;   10
each one has a promise of gold
and will return wealthy.

Instead of the mournful tune –
Donald Ban MacCrimmon's Lament –
the piper on board   15
incites the lads to dance and merriment.

The vessel is without canvas, without sails,
but, with engines fired,
she rends the mighty waves with her keel
and leaves them as mist behind her.   20

Toward the great wooded west
her prow is kept steady
by those who would not err in their course,
the sons of Islay and Mull.

One can be heard singing the praises   25
of the company lands unlimited
on which all minds and eyes are intent,
which we are fast approaching.[4]

'Us neach eile 'g inns' mu'n fhonn
30 A tha saor, farsuinn, torrach;
'Us a leithid éigneach lom
Tha an Alb' chreagach, chorrach.

Soraidh leibh, a chuideachd chaomh,
Tha Quebec nis am fradharc',
35 'S mar a sgapar moll le gaoth,
Bith sinn sgaoilte gu goirid.

'Us mur coinnich sinn gu bràth –
'Us 's e 's dòcha nach coinnich –
Cumaibh gaol ur n-òige blàth
40 Do thìr bhòidheach nam bonnach.

Another talks about the prairie
which is cheap, extensive, fertile,   30
contrasted with its counterpart, lean and bare,
in rocky, precipitous Scotland.

Farewell to you, kind friends,
Quebec is now in sight;
as chaff is scattered by the breeze   35
we shall soon be dispersed.

If we never meet again –
and most likely we shall not –
guard with ardour the love of your youth
for the fair land of the bannocks.   40

6 The Tradition Adapted

The foregoing is but a limited selection from an extensive and varied repertoire of emigration songs and poetry examined while preparing this edition. The genre takes many forms and draws on a wide range of circumstances and events. It would seem that almost invariably Highlanders regarded every change of residence as an occasion for a song or two. Consequently, it is not always easy to distinguish the songs of Gaels who went no farther than Glasgow or London from those of Gaels who emigrated to America or Asia.

That this particular song tradition persisted in new forms abroad, especially in Canada, is amply attested. As they moved from one area to another, Gaels in this country adapted it to their local circumstances, often with a refreshing note of humour and mild ridicule. The few random selections given here will serve to illustrate the vigour and diversity with which the genre took root and flourished in the New World.

It is well known that emigrants from the Highlands and the Western Isles who first settled in Upper Canada (Ontario) went on later to Manitoba and the Territories when the Canadian west was being colonized in the latter part of the nineteenth century.[1] John MacLean, a native of Balephuil, Tiree, emigrated to Upper Canada in 1878 and later took up residence far from kith and kin in Manitoba. The frontier was lonely but not without its challenge as illustrated in his *Oran do Mhanitôba* (*Song for Manitoba*).[2]

Cape Breton Gaels who 'emigrated' to Boston remembered the 'homeland' with nostalgia, as had their forbears when they put down on the wooded shores of Inverness County or Big Island in the nineteenth century. Boston was *Baile nam Beans* (*City of Beans*) to an anonymous Cape Bretoner in the 1920s who yearned for the sights and sounds of his native island.[3]

California had more to offer than Boston; yet the prosperous, verdant, and decadent land of his adoption was not entirely satisfying to another anonymous Gael of Cape Breton extraction. His *Duanag á California* (*Song from California*) reflects both the pleasant and unpleasant aspects of life there.[4] In the latter part of the song the bard describes his loneliness among so many unfriendly foreigners. He finds the heat oppressive, the women daring, and many people given to soft living. Yet he allows that those who are prudent and patient will ultimately prosper there.

ORAN DO MHANITOBA

Air allaban tha mi 's mi 'n dràsd an àit' ùr,
Nach deachaidh riamh àiteach, no bàrr thoirt á grunnd;
Ach 's e tha 'gam fhàgail-sa 'n dràsd air bheag sunnd,
Nach faic mi mo chàirdean air là na Bliadhn' Ur.

5 An uiridh an Canada bha sinn air dòigh,
Bha càirdean 's luchd-dùthcha gu dlùth air ar tòir;
Nis tha sinn air faondradh an taobh nach bu chòir,
Gun chaomh no gun charaid a rachadh 'nar còir.

Am fearann a th' againn 's ann ainneamh tha shamh'l,
10 Gun mhaide, gun chlach ann a bhacas an crann;
Cho fad' 's a bhios sinne mar Thìrisdich ann,
'S e Cnoc Mhic 'Illeathain bhios aige mar ainm.

Oidhche na Calluinn bha sinne gun sunnd,
Ach lean sinn am fasan a bh' againn bho thùs,

In Cape Breton, itself, what may be termed 'local emigration' elicited a number of songs in the same vein. One of the best known of these is by Alexander MacDonald (Ridge), who was born at Mabou and lived the latter part of his life at Lower South River, Antigonish County. In his *Duanag do Mhàbu* (*Song for Mabou*) the bard reminisces about the scenes and social activities of his beloved Mabou and resolves to visit his kin there now that the railroad has been built.[5]

Another such song, *Bràigh na h-Aibhne Deas* (*Upper South West River*), was doubtless intended as a parody on the emigration theme.[6] According to the song, the bard Angus MacDonald (Aonghas MacAlasdair) moved from his birthplace to Upper South West Mabou, a distance of about five miles, where he found himself estranged and even compelled to speak English, highly unlikely in that area in the 1860s.

SONG FOR MANITOBA

I am now a wanderer in this new land
which has never been inhabited, nor has it been tilled;
but what leaves me so dejected is that
I shall not see my friends on New Year's day.

Last year in Canada we were happy   5
with relatives and compatriots all around us.
Now we have strayed to a forbidding land,
without friend or relative to visit us.

The land which we now have, rare is its kind,
without stick or stone to obstruct the plough;   10
so long as we remain Tiree men here
MacLean's Hill will be its name.

New Year's eve we were low in spirit,
but we followed the custom which was ours from of old.

15 Bha mi 'n uiridh a gearain air là na Bliadhn' Ur;
'S ann agam am bliadhna tha reusan co-dhiù.

Ged tha sinn an dràsd fad' o'r càirdean gu léir,
Ma bhios iad a làthair, thig càch le'n toil fhéin,
'S nuair gheibh sinn an t-àite gu bàrr 'us gu feum
20 Cha bhi cuimhn' air na laithean a dh'fhàg sinn nar déigh.

BAILE NAM BEANS

O, 's ann tha mo ghaol-sa thall
Far an cluinnear gair nan allt,
'S iad a' ruith o àird nam beann
Tigh'nn nan deann gu Gleann na Maiseadh.

5 'S e 'n t-eilean beag is àirde prìs,
Siud far 'n d'àraicheadh mi-fhìn,
Far an cluinnear fuaim na pìob
Agus pìobaireachd le farum.

Siud an tìr 's am biodh an uall
10 Eadar froileagan 'us luaidh.
'S ged bha an geamhradh fuar
Cha bhiodh gruaman air na balaich.

Gur e mise tha gun phrìs
'S mi seo am 'Baile nam Beans,'
15 'S gun de dhachaidh agam fhìn
Ach rum bìdeach ann an *garret*.

DUANAG A CALIFORNIA

'S fhad' tha mi o m' dhùthaich fhéin;
Cha'n fhaigh thu na's fheàrr fo'n ghréin,

Last year I complained about New Year's day; 15
this year I have good reason to do so.

Though we are now far from all our friends,
if they are still living they will come out of their own will;
and when we have made the land productive
we shall forget the days bygone. 20

CITY OF BEANS

O, [the land of] my love is yonder,
where may be heard the gurgle of the streams
rushing down from the hills
and cascading into Glen Marsh.

It is in that small, most precious island 5
that I had my upbringing,
where could be heard the sound of the pipes
and piping of a high order.

That was the land of good cheer
with frolics and waulking bees; 10
although winter was cold
there was no gloom among the young.

Now I myself am of no worth
here in the 'City of Beans,'
with no home of my own 15
except a tiny room in a garret.

SONG FROM CALIFORNIA

Far am I from my own country;
you would find none better under the sun

Ged a shiubhladh tu air sgé
An saoghal gu taigh Iain Ghròta.

5   Bha mi uair 's bu mhór mo dhùil
Gu'm bithinn sona 'n corr dhe m' shaogh'l
Na'm bithin an dùthaich inntinneach, ùr,
'S gun ghaoth o'n tuath 'gam leònadh.

Gu fìrinneach tha 'n dùthaich àlainn,
10   'N àm a' gheamhraidh grìan cur blàths oirnn;
Gach seòrsa meas 'us flùr a' fàs
'S a' sneachd air bharr nam beanntan.

Tha duilleach dubh-ghorm air na craobhan
Fad na bliadhna, 's air na luibhean;
15   Coinnspeich 's gach seòrsa cuileag
A' cur srann 'nar cluasan.

Chan eil miann air gual no connadh,
Gas a' brùchdadh as an talamh;
Mu'n gann an cuir thu ris an lasair
20   Bidh goil air poit bhuntàta.

'S ann mu dheireadh a' mhios Mhàirt
'S mi air sìol a chur 's a' ghàradh,
Sùil ga'n d'thug mi maduinn thràth
Bha smeòraichean ri biadh ann.

25   'Tha sinn dol d'ar dùthaich nàdurr'
Do Cheap Breatunn, 'n uair bhios blàths ann;
Cho math 's gum bi do bhiadh 's ar càil,
'S e bhoiteag dhonn as fheàrr leinn.'

Co aige 's fheàrr tha fios na smeòrach
30   Gu de 'n dùthaich 'm bòidhche samhradh?
Cha bhi sùrd orra gu ceòl
Gu'n ruig iad Gleann nam Pìobair.

even if you searched throughout
the world to John O'Groats.

At one time I had great hopes 5
that I should be content for the rest of my life
if I were in a pleasant, new land
far from the blast of the north wind.

Truly this country is beautiful;
in winter the sun warms us, 10
and every kind of fruit and flower grows
while snow rests on the mountain peaks.

Blue-green foliage on the trees
remains throughout the year, and grasses as well;
wasps and every kind of fly 15
hum about our ears.

There is no need of coal or firewood
for gas oozes from the earth;
scarcely does one light it
when the potato pot boils. 20

It was towards the end of March,
after I had planted seed in the garden,
that I looked out on an early morning
to see robins having a meal there.

'We are going to our native land, 25
to Cape Breton when it is warm there;
no matter how good your food and hearty our appetite
we prefer the brown earthworm.'

Who knows better than the robin
which country is most beautiful in summer? 30
They have little zest for song
until they reach Pipers' Glen.

Tha daoine 'n seo á Carolina,
Mecsico, Iapan, 'us Tìna,
35   Roinn á Eileanan Hawaii,
'Us corr á Calamasu.

Cha bhuanaich fear 's a shùilean dùinte;
Feumaidh e bhith 'n gnàth 'na dhùsgadh.
Tha móran ann a ni ar spùilleadh
40   Mur a bi sinn teòma.

B'annsa leam bhi measg nan Gàidheal
'S am bheil duinealas 'us blàth-fhuil,
Na bhi measg gach seòrsa nàisinn,
Daoine dàna, fuara.

45   Tha ionndruinn mhór orm air mo chàirdean,
Coimhearsnaich bha fialaidh, bàigheil,
Rianail agus glan 'nan nàdur,
Taghadh dhaoine diadhaidh.

Bi mi bruadar air an dachaidh,
50   'S mi 'nam dhùsgadh 'us 'nam chadal;
Saoilidh mi 'n uair thig a' mhaduinn
Gu'n cluinn mi sruth na h-aibhne.

Mi gun lùths le teas na gréine,
'N àm an t-samhraidh tha i béisteil;
55   Feumaidh mi mo luideag léine
Fhàsgadh ceann gach uaire.

Ach dé math do neach bhi gruamach?
'N t-àite 's nach bi teas bi fuachd ann;
Gun fhios c' dhiubh 's fheàr an reòdhadh cruaidh
60   Na teine dearg na gréine.

Tha chuid mhór de shluagh gach baile
Dol an còmhnuidh chon na mara,

There are people here from Carolina,
Mexico, Japan, and China,
Some from the Hawaiian Islands,   35
and others from Kalamazoo.

One will not prosper with his eyes closed;
he must be alert at all times.
There are many who will ruin us
if we are not on our guard.   40

I would prefer to be among Gaels
with their humanity and warmth
than among different nationalities,
bold, cold people.

I miss my friends very much,   45
neighbours who were generous, cordial,
peaceful, good-natured,
the best of godly men.

I dream of home
When I am awake and when asleep;   50
I often think when morning comes
that I hear the rush of the river.

I am listless because of the hot sun;
in summer it is beastly.
I have to wring out   55
my bit of a shirt every hour.

But what good is it for one to be dissatisfied?
Where there is no heat there is cold.
One knows not which is better – the cruel frost
or the burning heat of the sun.   60

Most of the people of each city
go to the beach [and] habitually

'Slapaireachd bho thràth 's an latha
Gus an tig an oidhche.

65 Tha na nìonagan gun nàire
Ciadan dhiubh a' snàmh 's an t-sàile;
Iad mar na faoileagan bàna
luirg-ruist gu na sleisdean.

'N té tha nis a' dol gu dannsa
70 Cha bhi dh'aodach oirr' ach amharus;
'S ann as fheàrr a ni i 'n tango,
Trotan sionnuich, 's Charleston.

Fear tha gléidhteach agus cùr'mach,
Cha tig dad ris anns an dùthaich,
75 Ach mar d'rinn e fiar 's an tiormachd
'S ann as triume 'n lòd air.

Tha móran de na daoine dòigheil,
Cunntais mhór gun dad de chorr ac'.
Fear nach do dh'fhuaigh 'n toll 'na phòca
80 Tha e 'n taigh an dìgein.

Comhairle bheirinn air gach balach
Mu tha aige criomag baile,
Oibreachadh air ochd uair 's an latha
'S gheibh e fiach a shaothrach.

85 'S coma c'àite 'm bith mac an duine
Ged bhiodh crùn air air a mhullach,
Chan eil e 'n dàn dha a bhith buidheach
Ged bu leis an saoghal.

Fear tha deònach air bhi striochte
90 Ged bu daonnan air a riasladh
'S ann as fheàrr a chor 's an t-siorrachd
Ach e dh'fhulang faigh'd'neach.

lounge around from early morn
until nightfall.

The lassies are shameless,   65
hundreds of them bathing in the sea.
They are like the seagulls
barelegged to the thigh.

The one who now goes to a dance
is clothed with but a mere suggestion;   70
thus she can best do the tango,
the foxtrot, and the charleston.

The one who is thrifty and prudent
will not suffer in this country;
but if he didn't make hay in the dry weather   75
his load would be all the heavier.

Many of the folks here are well off,
a great many have just enough.
He who didn't mend the hole in his pocket
is in the poor house.   80

I would advise any young man
who has even a small bit of land
to work it eight hours a day
and his efforts will be fruitful.

It matters not where man finds himself,   85
even though a crown be on his head;
he is not destined to be completely happy
even if he had the whole world.

He who cheerfully accepts hardship,
although it be a constant struggle,   90
will fare better in eternity
if he but endure patiently.

DUANAG DO MHABU

'S e fàth mo mhulaid gun d'fhàs mi duilich
'N uair dh'fhàg mi buileach an t-àite.
Gur h-ann mu thuath, taobh thall a' chuain
Tha 'n t-eilean 'san d'fhuair mi m' àrach.

5   Gun d'shil mo shùil aig meud mo thùirs',
'N uair rinn mi 'n dùthaich fhàgail.
Is e thug m' àbhachd bhuam 's mo shunnd
Mi chur mo chùl ri Màbu.

'Us far an d'àraicheadh mi 'n tus,
10 Bu mhùirneach bha mo chàirdean;
'Us thar gach àit' an d'fhuair mi iùl
Gun tug mi rùn do Mhàbu.

Is beag an t-ìoghnadh ged a liath mi,
B' iargainneach gach là mi.
15 Sud an turn a dh'fhàg mi cianail,
Mi thigh'nn riamh á Màbu.

Ann am leabaidh na mo dhùisg,
'S mi caoidh na dùthch' a dh'fhàg mi,
Saoilidh mi gum faic mo shùil
20 Gach cnoc 'us lub tha 'm Màbu.

Bu tric a choisich mi le sùrd
A null gu ceann an t-sàile;
Far am faighteadh mire 's mùirn
Le sunnd aig Drochaid Mhàbu.

25 Bhiomaid cridheil ann air bhainnsean,
'N t-àm a rinn mi fhàgail.
Gheibhteadh ceòl ann agus dram
'Us danns' air ùrlar clàraidh.

SONG FOR MABOU

The cause of my grief is that I became sad
when I left the place for good.
North across the sea
is the island where I was brought up.

My grief was such that my eyes shed tears   5
when I left that country.
What has sapped my joy and my spirit
is that I turned my back on Mabou.

Where I was raised in my youth
my friends were very cheerful;   10
and of all places that I knew
my great love was Mabou.

Little wonder that I have greyed
for I was sorrowful every day.
The turn [of events] which made me sad   15
was that I ever left Mabou.

In my bed when I awake,
mourning for the land that I left,
I imagine that my eyes see
every hill and pond in Mabou.   20

Often did I walk eagerly
over to the bay
where there would be mirth and merriment
resounding at Mabou Bridge.

We would be jolly there at weddings   25
at the time I took my leave.
There would be music and drink
and dancing on the board floor.

C'àit' bheil an òigridh ghrinn sin
30 A bhiodh leinn an tràth ud?
'S beag nach eil gach aon a chinn diù
Anns a' chill fo'n fhàilein.

Bho na fhuair iad rathad iarainn
Ni mi triall gun dàil ann
35 A shealltuinn na bheil beò de'n t-sìol
A dh'fhàg mi shios am Màbu.

Nise sguiridh mi de m' dhuan,
Oir 's ceaird gun bhuaidh a' bhàrdachd;
Ach gu bràth cha toir mu fuath
40 Do'n tìr 'san d'fhuair mi m' àrach.

BRAIGH NA H-AIBHNE A DEAS

Tha mise brònach 's mi 'n seo 'nam aonrachd
'S mi 'gabhail òranan le cridhe trom;
'S e chleachd mi còmhlan a shuidheadh còmhl' rium,
A ghabhadh òrain 's a thogadh fonn.
5 Fear a'chòmhraidh gum faict' aig bòrd e,
B'e siud a'chòmhdhail a chòrdadh rium
'S gum b'annsa móran a bhi siud còmhl' riu
Na 'n seo a' còmhnaidh am measg nan ròl.

Cha'n ìoghnadh dhomhsa ged bhithinn cràiteach
10 Am baille Thearlaich cho fada shuas;
Cha ruig mo chàirdean mi mar a b'àbhaist
Anns an tràth seo a' ghabhail dhuan.
Ag ionndruinn tha mi na fir a dh'fhàg mi
Aig an robh an cànain dha'n tug mi luaidh;
15 'S nach cluinn mi 'n dràsda na bhruidhneas Gàidhlig
Ach *Peter* Dhabhaidh 's a bhràthair ruadh.

Dhomh-sa is fheudar dol ris a' bheurla
Ged nach réidh thig i chum mo bheòil.

Where are the fine youths
who were with us at that time?   30
Most likely each of them who grew up there
is now in the churchyard under the sod.

Since the railroad has come
I shall go without delay
to see those still living of the kin   35
whom I left down in Mabou.

Now I shall cease my song
for poetry is a useless art;
but never shall I disdain
the land where I had my upbringing   40

UPPER SOUTH WEST RIVER

I am sad and lonely here
singing songs with heavy heart;
I was used to friends who would sit with me
and sing songs and join in chorus.
A boon companion, seen at table,   5
was the company most pleasing to me.
I much preferred to be with that kind
then to dwell here among the rabble.

Small wonder that I am so dejected
on Charles' farm so far up yonder;   10
My friends cannot reach me as usual
now to sing songs.
I miss those I left behind
for they had the language which I love.
Now I hear no one who speaks Gaelic   15
except Peter David and his red-haired brother.

I am compelled to turn to English
although I have no facility with it.

Rium cha'n éisd iad ag innse sgeula,
20 Tha mi mar chreutair bhiodh ann an ceò.
Ged bhios mi strì ris an aghaidh m' inntinn
Gur nàrach dìblidh a bhios mo ghlòir;
'S e an cànain prìseil a bh' aig mo shinnsear
'S am b'fheàrr a dh'innsinn dhaibh brìgh mo sgeul.

25 Bho'n thriall mi 'n taobh seo 's a liath an aois mi
Gun tug mi aomadh a chum an làir;
Cha ghluais mi aotram 's mi tric a' smaointean,
A chaoidh, nach fhaod mi bhi mar a bha.
A' chuibhle ghluais mi le car gun bhuannachd
30 'S a chuir 's an uair seo mi anns an àit',
Nach fhaic mi bhuam as ach barran fuaraidh
'S an chuid as suaraiche ann a' fàs.

Solus gréine chan fhaic mi-fhéin ann
, 'S ann tha na speuran cho tiugh le neòil.
35 Maduinn chéitein an tim dhomh éiridh
An leus cha léir dhomh leis a'cheò.
Tha 'n diugh gach creutair a' ruith a' chéile
Gur chulaidh-oillt iad air feadh an fheòir;
A' nathair bhéisteil 's an cràigean déisneach
40 A chì mi 'us greim aic' air a spòig.

Gur mór an ann-tlachd tha 'm blàths an t-samhraidh;
Gluaisidh gach fann-chreutair, thig iad beò.
A' chuileag lann-gheur 'us móran ann dhiù
Gum fad' an geall air bhi ann am fheòil.
45 Ged tha i suarach cha chreid an sluagh bhuam
A' mhiad 's a' bhuaireadh th'ann sa phòr;
'S a dh' aindeòin suathaidh cha chum mi bhuam iad
'S gun àt mo chluasan cho tiugh ri bòrd.

'S e liath cho tràth mi gun thriall na laithean
50 'S gach fasan Gàidhealach air dhol air chùil;
Ged phòsadh càiread cha thachair càirdean
Gu coibhneil, bàigheil mar bha air thùs.

They will not listen to me when I tell stories;
I am like a poor creature in a fog.   20
Although I try, contrary to my inclination,
shamefully halting is my speech.
It is in the precious tongue of my ancestors
that I can best convey the essence of my tales.

Since I have wandered here and have greyed with age   25
I have suffered a decline;
I cannot move lightly, and often I think,
alas, that I can never be as I used to.
Alas for the wheel that moved me with an unfortunate turn
and put me here now,   30
from where I can see only the cold mountains yonder,
and where only the most worthless things grow.

I cannot see the light of the sun here
for the sky is thick with clouds.
On a May morning when I get up   35
I see nothing because of the fog.
Today every creature attacks another,
a disgusting matter, in the hay;
the horrid snake and the helpless frog
I see with its legs in her grasp.   40

Great is the discomfort in the heat of summer;
every miserable creature comes to life.
The fly with its sharp sting, and there are many of them,
has long since had designs on my flesh.
Although it is insignificant, people will not believe   45
the degree of distress of which the species is capable.
And regardless of lotions I cannot ward them off
and my ears swell as thick as boards.

What has greyed me so early in life is the passing of time
and every Gaelic custom abandoned.   50
Although a couple might get married friends will not gather
cordially, faithfully as of old.

An stuth a b' àille chuir as an àite,
Gu bheil an dràsda oirnn fanntas ùr.
55   Gur h-ainneamh iad-san, a chum na bha dhiù,
'S chan aobhar gàire a th' anns a' chùis.

Numerous other examples could be adduced to illustrate the popularity of the emigration theme among Gaels several removes from the homeland. Indeed, almost every Highland community across Canada had its local bards, Gaels like Alexander MacLean (Alasdair MacEoghain) of River Denys, Cape Breton, who could match his erstwhile peers by his remarkable powers of invective as well as by his nostalgic eloquence. A turn of the century figure, he is still remembered in Inverness County as one whose name was synonymous with impromptu Gaelic satire. Many of his songs were highly provocative and the contents offensive to many people; those who knew them learned them in secret and would not risk singing them at social gatherings lest they pro-

The most delightful drink has been banned from the place
and now we are faint-hearted again.
Rare are those [friends], no matter how numerous they used to
  be;   55
cheerless indeed is the state of affairs.

---

voke a storm. Consequently they are now known to very few people.

Even a brief look at the output of men such as Alasdair MacEoghạin suggests that much interesting and illuminating material, relevant to the Scottish Canadian scene, remains virtually unknown. Clearly, this particular cultural transplant merits further serious research as a significant component of the Canadian mosaic. Notwithstanding the decline of Gaelic during the past few decades, the current resurgence of interest in ethnicity and the long overdue respectability now accorded the language give promise that such research might materialize in the not too distant future.

AIRS

ABBREVIATIONS AND
SELECT BIBLIOGRAPHY

NOTES

INDEXES

Airs

Only a limited number of the airs of the songs in this collection can be identified with reasonable certainty. The elusive nature of the oral tradition and more especially the decline of the Gaelic-singing tradition among third and fourth generation Gaels abroad render the search for such airs almost fruitless. The selections tend to fall into three categories.

1 Songs whose airs are indicated in the printed sources, and those whose texts suggest a familiar air to which they may be sung.
2 A small number recorded in recent times.
3 A number for which it has not been possible to obtain airs thus far.

Such transcriptions of 1 and 2 as were accessible are given here.

SGEULA A FHUAIR MI BHO DHI-DOMHNUICH

Air: Not indicated in the printed sources, but may be sung to the above air, taken from *The Airs and Melodies peculiar to the Highlands of Scotland and the Isles*, ed Captain Simon Fraser of Knockie (Edinburgh 1816), no 45, p 26

BHO NA SGUIR MI PHAIDHEADH MAIL

Air: Taken from Fraser, *Airs and Melodies*, no 226, p 102, where it is identified as *Ho cha neil mulad oirn* (*The Emigrant's Adieu*). In a note on p 119 the editor states: 'The sentiments conveyed by the words of John McMurdo, or McRae of Kintail, formerly mentioned as having emigrated, most feelingly point out the proper resources of the mind, in bearing the adversities of life.'

NISE BHO NA THACHAIR SINN

Air: The refrain suggests that this song was sung to the well known air of *Tha tighinn fodham, fodham, fodham*. There is an early transcription of this air in Alexander Campbell's *Albyn's Anthology*, I and II (Edinburgh 1816-18), 63. The variant below is from Fraser, *Airs and Melodies*, no 225, p 102.

DEAN CADALAN SAMHACH

Air: This lullaby was recorded by John Lorne Campbell of Canna in Cape Breton in 1937, and transcribed by Seumas Ennis of the Irish Folklore Commission in 'A Collection of Folksongs and Music,' no 95. It is reproduced here with the kind permission of Dr Campbell and of the Head of the Department of Irish Folklore, University College, Dublin.

O, 'S ALAINN AN T-AITE

Air: Also recorded by John Lorne Campbell in Nova Scotia in 1937, and transcribed by Seumas Ennis in 'A Collection of Folksongs and Music,' no 133. Reproduced here also with permission as above.

AM MEALLADH

Air: 'Hugaibh air nigh'n donn nam meall-shuil'; taken from K.N. MacDonald, *The Gesto Collection of Highland Music* (Leipzig 1895), 10

MOLADH AGUS SORAIDH CHOMHAIL

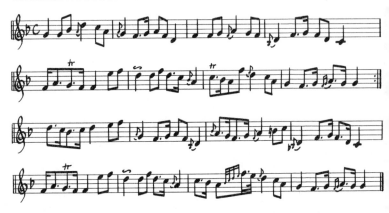

Air: Fraser, *Airs and Melodies*, no 209, p 96 as above. Variants are published in Patrick MacDonald, *A Collection of Highland Vocal Airs* (Edinburgh 1784), 21, and *An Gaidheal* III (1874), 19

O, SIUD AN TAOBH A GHABHAINN

Air: Transcribed from *Orain-Aon-Neach*, Leabhar VI (Oban 1953), 20, and reproduced here with permission from An Comunn Gàidhealach. The air was collected in Cape Breton from Stephen Black by the late Annie Johnston of Barra in 1953.

TEIST DHOMHNAILL AIR MANITOBA

Air: Sung to the air of *Hi ri ri o rathill o / 'S i nighean donn as boidhche*. This air is well known in Cape Breton where it was collected by Major C.I.N. MacLeod from Mr and Mrs Archie MacMaster, Port Hastings, Inverness County, in 1956. Later it was transcribed by Harold Hamer and published in *Gaelic Songs in Nova Scotia*, ed Helen Creighton and Calum MacLeod (Ottawa 1964), 34. Reproduced here with permission from the National Museum of Man, National Museums of Canada

Abbreviations and Select Bibliography

An t-Oranaiche Archibald Sinclair, *An T-Oranaiche* (Glasgow 1870)

Casket The Casket, a weekly paper published at Antigonish, Nova Scotia, since 1852

Clarsach Clarsach na Coille, ed by the Reverend Alexander Maclean Sinclair, revised by Hector MacDougall (Glasgow 1928)

Campbell, H.F., 'Donald Matheson and other Gaelic Poets in Kildonan,' *TGSI* XXIX (1914-19), 134-43

Campbell, James C.M., Biographical Notes on the life of John Macrae. Middlesex, England ca 1966

CM Celtic Magazine 1875-88

'A Collection of Folksongs and Music made in Nova Scotia in 1937 by John Lorne Campbell, together with songs and music gathered by Margaret Fay Shaw Campbell in the Outer Isles of Scotland. Transcriptions by Seumas Ennis.' Original manuscript in possession of Roinn Bhéaloideas Éireann, University College, Dublin

Douglas, Thomas Earl of Selkirk, *Observations on the present state of the Highlands of Scotland with a view to the Causes and Probable Consequences of Emigration* 2nd ed (Edinburgh 1806)

Dwelly, Edward *Illustrated Gaelic-English Dictionary* 6th ed (Glasgow 1967)

Failte Cheap-Breatuin, ed Vincent A. McLellan. Printed edition 1890 reissued in typescript by James H. McNeil (Sydney 1933)

Filidh na Coille Filidh na Coille: Dain agus Orain Leis a'Bhard Mac-Gilleain agus le Feadhainn

Eile, ed by the Reverend Alexander Maclean Sinclair (Charlottetown 1901)

Gaelic Bards Three of the four volumes edited under this title by the Reverend Alexander Maclean Sinclair: *The Gaelic Bards from 1715 to 1765* (Charlottetown 1892); *The Gaelic Bards from 1765 to 1825* (Sydney 1896); *The Gaelic Bards from 1825 to 1875* (Sydney 1904)

Gairm Gaelic quarterly published at Glasgow since 1952

Grimble, Ian, 'Emigration in the time of Rob Donn, 1714-1778,' *Scottish Studies* VII (1963), 129-53

Highland Songs of the Forty-Five, ed John Lorne Campbell (Edinburgh 1933)

Laoidhean Spioradail le Domhnull Mathanach, ed by John MacDonald and John Kennedy (Pictou 1832)

Lord Selkirk's Diary 1803-1804, ed P.C.T. White (Toronto 1958)

MT Mac-Talla, a Gaelic newspaper, ed by Jonathan MacKinnon (Sydney 1892-1904)

Ridge mss Unpublished manuscripts of Allan MacDonald (the Ridge), np, nd; originals in the library of St Francis Xavier University, Antigonish

SGS Scottish Gaelic Studies

SHR Scottish Historical Review

TGSI Transactions of the Gaelic Society of Inverness

Notes

Introduction

1 See the Introduction to his
   *Highland Songs of the Forty-
   Five* (Edinburgh 1933) xvii-
   xxviii.

2 Alexander Carmichael, 'Deir-
   dire,' *TGSI* XIII (1886-7), 251.
   The oldest extant version of
   this quatrain is in the Glen-
   masan Manuscript, probably
   transcribed in the fifteenth
   century from an earlier text;
   see Whitley Stokes, 'The Sons
   of Uisneach,' *Irische Texte*, ed
   W. Stokes and E. Windisch
   (Leipzig 1887), II, 107.

3 *A Celtic Miscellany*, ed K.H.
   Jackson (Edinburgh 1951),
   307-8. Jackson dates it as
   twelfth century, author unknown.

4 General summaries are given
   by F. Fraser Darling in *West*
   Highland Survey (London
   1955), 1-6, and G.S. Pryde, *A*
   History of Scotland (Edinburgh 1962), II, 150-61.

5 *The Making of the Crofting*
   Community (Edinburgh 1976)

6 Hunter, 9

7 Campbell, *Songs*, xxii

8 Campbell, *Songs*, 142, 143

9 Hunter, 11; my italics

10 Generally this was so, but
    when the estates were re-
    stored in the 1780s some
    tacksmen were restored as
    well.

11 Hunter, 13

12 Important sources are: Tho-
    mas Telford, *Survey and*
    Report of the Coast and Central
    Highlands of Scotland, made
    by the command of the Right
    Honourable, the Lords Com-
    missioners of His Majesty's
    Treasury in the autumn of

1802, *Parliamentary Reports. 1802-1803* IV; Thomas Douglas, Earl of Selkirk, *Observations on the present state of the Highlands of Scotland with a view to the Causes and Probable Consequences of Emigration* (Edinburgh 1806). Among the more useful recent studies are the essays of M.I. Adam, 'The Highland Emigration of 1770,' *SHR* XVI (1919), 280-93, and 'The Causes of Highland Emigration, 1783-1803,' *SHR* VII (1920), 73-89; also Ian Grimble, 'Emigration in the time of Rob Donn,' *Scottish Studies* VII (1963), 129-53.

13 Hunter, 13

14 *John Home's Survey of Assynt*, ed R.J. Adam and K.M. MacIver (Edinburgh 1960), xxxv

15 For North Uist see *The Songs of John MacCodrum*, ed William Matheson (Edinburgh 1938), 314; for the other areas, M.I. Adam, 'The Eighteenth Century Landlords and the Poverty Problem,' *SHR* XIX (1921-2), 10.

16 See Viola R. Cameron, *Emigration from Scotland to America 1874-75* (Baltimore 1959); in addition to increased rents, the emigrants complained about the scarcity of bread because of the great quantities of corn used for distillation; p 13.

17 See especially the essays of M.I. Adam cited above; Telford, *Report*, 15; Gray, 86-104; and Gordon Donaldson, *The Scot Overseas* (London 1956), 52-4.

18 *Strictures and Remarks on the Earl of Selkirk's Observations on the present state of the Highlands* (Edinburgh 1806)

19 *SHR* XVII (1920), 83

20 For a thorough discussion of the kelping industry see chapter 2 in *The Making of the Crofting Community* 14 ff.

21 Donaldson, 78-9

22 Darling, 5

23 Iain N. MacLeòid, *Bàrdachd Leòdhais* (Glasgow 1916), 138, from a song by Murchadh Mac a' Ghobhainn (Murdoch Smith), a late nineteenth-century Gaelic bard.

24 James Boswell, *The Journal of a Tour to the Hebrides* (Oxford 1924), 267

25 For Sutherland and Strathglass, see below pp 19-21 and 60-5 respectively. The misery endured under Gordon of Cluny is documented on both sides of the Atlantic. In 1849 John MacEachern, a native of South Uist, sailed on the *Mount Stuart* with about four hundred other Uist emigrants destined for Middlesex county, Ontario.

MacEachern left a very interesting account of the circumstances which preceded the exodus. All small tenants were forced to sell their cattle for about $1.00 a head and leave the county. Only a very small number spoke any English at all. Many were ill on the way and many more died. Some time after their arrival twelve of these emigrant families left Middlesex county and took up residence in Huron county, Michigan. Five of the men who came out originally in 1849 were still living there in 1906 when John MacEachern's account was collected and published in the *Detroit News* on 27 July of that year.

26 Ian C. Graham, *Colonists from Scotland* (Ithaca 1956), 58 ff; *Songs of John MacCodrum*, 314; Donaldson, 59; *Survey of Assynt*, xxvi, n 83

27 *Survey of Assynt*, xxx, n 101

28 *SHR* xix (1921-2), 7: 'As late as 1808 about 40,000 persons were still sub-tenants in the Hebrides ... and in Sutherland indirect tenure was still the normal' status of the people.

29 Donaldson, 51. A thorough investigation of the status of the tacksmen on the Argyle estates has been published by E.R. Cregeen, 'The Tacksmen and their Successors: A Study of Tenurial Reorganization in Mull, Morven, and Tiree in the early 18th Century,' *Scottish Studies* xiii (1969), 93-144.

30 *SHR* xix (1921-2), 12; *Survey of Assynt*, xxxi, n 106

31 The duties of the factor have been described by R.C. MacLeod in an article based on Estate Regulations mss, 1769, preserved at Dunvegan: 'A West Highland Estate during Three Centuries,' *SHR* xxii (1925), 161-81.

32 First published in *Blackwood's Edinburgh Magazine* (September 1829)

33 Some of the earliest reports came from North Carolina; extracts from these are contained in 'Agriculture in North Carolina' by W. Neil Franklin, in *North Carolina Historical Review* iii (1926), 539-74. In 1773 'Scotus Americanus' addressed his 'Informations Concerning the Province of North Carolina' to emigrants from the Highlands; this document was published by W.K. Boyd in *Some Eighteenth Century Tracts Concerning North Carolina* (Raleigh 1927), 420 ff.

34 The complete text of the song is edited below, pp 32-4.

35 See page 26 below, lines 95-6.

36 *The Cape Breton Advocate*, I, 4 (16 September 1840), 26

37 *The MacDonald Collection of Gaelic Poetry*, ed A. and A. MacDonald (Inverness 1911), 370-1

38 For accounts of wretched condition on emigrant vessels see Telford, *Report*, Appendix A, 35-7, and Oliver Mac-Donagh's excellent study, *A Pattern of Government Growth 1800-1860* (London 1961). MacDonagh attributes the enactment of the first of the Passenger acts (1803) to Telford's *Report*. In 1894 Malcolm Ferguson contributed to *Mac-Talla* a complete Gaelic account of his voyage from Tobermory to Cape Breton on the *Neith* in 1843. The ship had been engaged by Mac-Niven, who persuaded the emigrants, most of whom were from South Uist, to leave the country. After a hasty preparation, the party set out in the very leaky vessel and spent perilous days at sea before they were obliged to return to Belfast where a better vessel was then provided; *MT* II, 49 (1894), 2-3.

39 In an exceptionally beautiful work, *The World of the Vikings* (London 1967), Ole Klindt Jensen remarks (pp 10-11) that the Norsemen gave ships fanciful names such as keel-bird and sea-horse, as illustrated in part of his quotation from the poetry of Sigrat Thordsson: 'The sea-horse ran in glory, / She planed the brine with her keel.'

40 P 68, below, lines 21-4

41 *MT* II, 49 (1894), 3

42 Telford, *Report*, Appendix (D), 41: passengers leaving the Highlands and Islands were said to have taken £100,000 sterling with them in the period 1801-2.

43 P 90, below, lines 36-40

44 *Filidh na Coille*, 194-5

45 *Clarsach*, 314-6

46 Samuel Johnson, *A Journey to the Western Islands of Scotland* (Oxford 1924), 53

47 The term 'bard' is used throughout this work since Gaels in exile so designated all those among them who composed songs and/or Gaelic verse.

48 The most notable collector in Scotland was the late Calum MacLean. No tribute can adequately cover the extent and value of his work in the field. Hundreds of songs and folk-tales which he recovered and recorded all over Scotland are now in the archives of the School of Scottish Studies, Edinburgh. Another scho-

larly pioneer collector is the present laird of Canna, John Lorne Campbell. He and his wife, Margaret Fay Shaw, have been engaged for over forty years in recovering as much as possible of the Gaelic literary heritage before it vanishes with the present generation of Gaelic informants. Of great interest and value is the collection made by Professor C.W. Dunn, chairman of the department of Celtic languages and literatures of Harvard University. This collection represents various parts of Cape Breton and other Gaelic areas in Canada, including Glengarry county, Ontario, and the eastern townships of Quebec. It is now deposited in the Celtic Archives, Boylston Hall, Harvard University.

49 *Songs of John MacCodrum*, 196-203 and 132-44
50 Standard editions are in *Clarsach*, 90-4, and *Filidh na Coille*, 48-52.
51 The succinct statement by Derick S. Thomson in his recent work, *An Introduction to Gaelic Poetry* (London 1974), 15, reads in part: 'There is no complete substitute for appreciation of poetry in a particular language short of learning that language and learning it well. In particular there are many examples of verbal wit that can hardly be fully translated, for they may often depend on the whole range of a word's connotations, and there is only one kind of computer, to date, that can be programmed in the right way to appreciate this. In similar fashion, humour of situation and humour of character often depend for their effect on a knowledge of the culture's stereos, and an intimate knowledge at that.'

Chapter 1: The Carolinas

DONALD MATHESON

1 Brief biographical notes are given in a preface to *Laoidhean Spioradail*, 27-30, which appears to be an exact copy of the second edition of Donald Matheson's poetry, probably published in Tain in 1825. For further details about the bard see H.F. Campbell, 'Donald Matheson and other Gaelic Poets in Kildonan,' *TGSI* XXIX (1914-19), 134-43, and Grimble, n 12, p 000 above.
2 Campbell remarks that for five centuries after Gilbert,

bishop of Caithness, had translated the Psalms in the thirteenth century, the literary records of Caithness and Sutherland were singularly sterile.

3 The influence of the bard's satires as well as their sprightliness and charming melody is noted by the Reverend Donald MacLean in 'The Literature of the Scottish Gael,' *Celtic Review* VIII (1912-13), 66.

4 See Grimble, 137, where the circumstances of the two poets are contrasted: Matheson witnessed the incipient social upheaval in Sutherland, while Rob Donn enjoyed the relative security of the Reay country, the part of Strathnaver which was under the MacKay.

5 The consolidation of the estates of Sutherland was secured by the shrewd Lady of Strathnaver, grandmother of Earl William. After the death of the earl, the young countess was brought up in Edinburgh. Her claim to the estates was not officially established until 1771 (Grimble, 137). In the interim the factors who managed them did so to their own advantage. The *Survey of Assynt* indicates the extent of the

surveys carried out in that part of the earldom during this period and the consequences to the tenantry.

6 Campbell, 138

7 See Alexander Hewatt, *An Historical Account of the Rise and Progress of the Colonies of South Carolina and Georgia* II (London 1779), 269; two townships were laid out, one on the Savanah river at Mecklenburgh, the other at Londonderry on the Santee. There is also a note in *Songs of John MacCodrum*, 314, to the effect that, after the rise in rents on North Uist in 1769, several tacksmen grouped together in protest and bought 10,000 acres in South Carolina, to which they and their tenants emigrated shortly afterwards.

8 Such was Hewatt's account of the good fortune of those who had arrived at an early date in South Carolina, as related in *Historical Account*, 303. Hewatt had returned to Scotland in 1776 when the threat of revolution became imminent. In addition to his own observations, it is likely that he was assisted in writing his account by Governor Bull who was a friend of his and exceptionally well in-

formed, having been governor continuously from 1746. South Carolina is described as a 'Contentious Commonwealth Just South of Eden' by Louis B. Wright in *South Carolina* (New York, 1976), 16-29.

9 Campbell, 136
10 *Laoidhean Spioradail*, 27-30
11 There is a Gaelic note added to the text which specifies that the reference is to the young children who had recently succeeded the Earl of Sutherland and Lord Reay.
12 'Iomairt' also means 'struggle' so an alternate rendering would be 'when the struggle was difficult.'
13 This line seems to imply a fear of the sea; a more accurate rendering might be 'I wouldn't go very far.'
14 'dàn mar dhùrachd' is glossed in the text as 'having according to wish,' *Laoidhean Spioradail*, 29. I have followed the rendering given by Grimble, 140.

JOHN MACRAE

1 Biographical details and a genealogy are given by the Reverend Alexander Maclean Sinclair in *MacTalla nan Tur* (Sydney, Nova Scotia, 1901),

54. See also Alexander MacKenzie, 'John Macrae – Iain MacMhurchaidh – the Kintail Bard,' *CM* VII (1882), 271-6, 322-5, 387-9, 426-8; Colin Chisholm, 'Unpublished Old Gaelic Songs,' *TGSI* XII (1885-6), 144-52; the Reverend Alexander Macrae, *History of the Clan Macrae* (Dingwall 1899), 81-3 and 402-7.
2 *TGSI* XII (1885-6), 147
3 *CM* VII (1882), 426
4 Donald F. MacDonald, 'A Tar Heel Gaelic Bard,' *Souvenir Program and Review* Twelfth Annual Grandfather Mountain Highland Games (North Carolina 1967), 11.
5 Macrae, *History*, 83
6 *TGSI* XII (1885-6), 144
7 Macrae, *History*, 83
8 In the song *'S mi air fògradh bho fhoghair*, edited below, pp 50-4. On 3 May 1776, Cornwallis entered the mouth of Cape Fear, where a formidable British naval force had already assembled. The force was too large to be of service on the coast of North Carolina but, before moving on towards Charleston, Cornwallis was deputed to go ashore with 900 men to lay waste the town of Brunswick: H.B. Carrington, *Battles of the American Revolution* (New

York 1876), 174-5. Cornwallis returned to North Carolina in 1780-1. Macrae's song suggests prolonged hardship and exile, and it more likely refers to this latter coming than to that of 1776.

9 Information in a letter from the Reverend James MacKenzie, Olivia, North Carolina, 22 January 1969, taken from *Cumberland Deed Records*, Book F (6), 351.

10 Also from the letter in n 9. The claim was filed by Dr Alexander Morrison, and it included a letter from his son, Norman, who had returned to North Carolina to check on his father's relatives who were still there. It is to this letter that we owe the brief description of McLendon's Creek in 1784.

11 It seems reasonable to conclude that the correspondent was the Reverend John Bethune whose mother resided at McLendon's Creek. There is considerable information about this royalist missionary prior to his emigration and for the post-revolutionary period. He is known to have been chaplain in General MacDonald's army at Moore's Creek. After a brief imprisonment, he went to Halifax, Nova Scotia, where he served with the Royal Highland Emigrant Regiment. In 1782 he went to Montreal and sometime later he went on to Glengarry. He became the first Presbyterian minister in Upper Canada and died at Williamstown on 23 September 1815. See the *Presbyterian News* (North Carolina Synod, December 1965), 8-9.

12 First published in Glasgow in 1841.

13 *CM* VII (1882), 271-6. It is interesting to note that their publication drew a response from F.D. MacDonell, Te Ante, Hawke's Bay, New Zealand who stated that he knew all of the Macrae songs which were published in *CM* in 1882. He contributed another, *B'fheàrr leam gu'n cluinninn uaibh sgeula*, which appeared in *CM* VIII (1883), 464: text and translation are given below, pp 32-4.

14 *TGSI* XII (1885-6), 147: one of these describes his role in a 'réiteach' (marriage proposal) in Strathglass.

15 *TGSI* XII (1885-6), 118. For the Dornie manuscripts see Angus Matheson, 'Gleanings from the Dornie Manuscripts,' *TGSI* XLI (1951-2), 310-81.

16 Notes from Loyalist claims in

North Carolina Department of Archives and History, in a letter from the Reverend James MacKenzie, 12 February 1969.

17 Macrae, *History*, 405

18 Exact dates of his compositions are unknown; those from North Carolina must have been contemporary with the American Revolution. There is a note in *MT* III, 4 (1895), 8, which states that Michael MacDonald, captain and poet, who came to Prince Edward Island in 1772, composed a song during the winter which he spent alone in Judique, Nova Scotia. Local tradition has it that the year was 1775.

19 Text: *CM* VIII (1883), 464

20 Texts: *CM* VII (1882), 388-9 and 323; Macrae, *History*, 402-3

21 Text: *CM* VII (1882), 322 and 388

22 Texts: *CM* VII (1882), 323-4 and 388; Macrae, *History*, 403-5. Malcolm MacLeod raised an 'Erse song ... *Hatyin, foam, foam eri'* to which he gave Jacobite words of his own as he rowed Boswell and Johnson across to Raasay on 8 September 1773; Boswell, *Journal*, 265.

23 Texts: *TGSI* XII (1885-6), 151-2; *NCHR* XXXVI (1959), 473-5, edited with notes and translation by Charles W. Dunn

24 *Casket* (9 March 1922), 11

25 The melody for this recording was transcribed by Seumas Ennis of the Irish Folklore Commission and published privately in *Collection of Folksongs and Music made in Nova Scotia and Canna* (copy in Special Collections of the library of St Francis Xavier University, Antigonish), no 95.

26 *Poetry of Badenoch* (Inverness 1906), 38-9

27 Texts: *CM* VII (1882), 464-6; *TGSI* XII (1885-6), 148-50; *MT* X (1902), 223. This song goes to the same tune as Duncan Ban MacIntyre's *Cumha Coire a' Cheathaich* (*Song to the Misty Corrie*). It is also reminiscent of it in content.

28 Information from Mrs Muirchison, a resident of Edinburgh in 1967, who claimed relationship to the bard.

29 Texts: *CM* VII (1882), 466-7; *TGSI* XII (1885-6), 152-3; *MT* X (1902), 216; Macrae, *History*, 405-7

30 This may refer to some kind of unfavourable notice from the landlords expected by spring.

31 The retainer no longer needed in the Highlands

32 As already remarked, several landlords had offered the bard a good farm if he would remain at home.

33 The custom of chartering ships is described by Selkirk in his *Observations*, 147: 'Whenever the circumstances of any part of the country induced the people to think of emigration, the usual procedure has generally been that the leading individuals have circulated a subscription paper, to which all those, who agreed to join in chartering a ship for the purpose, signed their names; and whenever they had thereby ascertained their number, they called together all those who had declared their intention to emigrate.'

34 The crab is associated with miserliness and usurpation; Dwelly, 716. Here the implication is that, unlike their predecessors, the new landlords have no scruple about displacing tenants if they deem it profitable to do so.

35 For a description of horses in the southern colonies at that time see Hewatt, *Historical Account*, 303.

36 Official concern about emigration is recorded in the Acts of the Privy Council of England, Colonial Series, VI (Lichenstein 1966), 508: Board of Trade Report, 24 June 1772. The Board 'in this case protests against the general and unlimited consideration by the Board of applications for lands in America, and expresses alarm at the increasing emigration from Great Britain and Ireland.'

37 The building of dykes was an obligation incumbent upon both tacksmen and their tenants. In the study by R.C. MacLeod, already cited, it is noted that the tacksman had to make up his share of the March dykes around his farm jointly with his neighbours; tenants were directed to enclose and subdivide the grounds of their farms, whether for corn or grass for the first twelve years of the lease. If this duty was not fulfilled, the rents were increased by twenty per cent. When a tenant left he was paid half of the expense incurred; see *SHR* XXII (1925), 165; also R.A. Gailey, 'Mobility of Tenants on a Highland Estate in the early Nineteenth Century,' *SHR* XL (1961), 136-45.

38 It is related that one spring Macrae's cattle perished in a snowstorm at Comhlan in Glen Affric. His response to the calamity was a spirited song; information from unpublished biographical notes on the life of John Macrae, by James C.M. Campbell (Middlesex, England, 1966).

39 Possibly the Cherokees, whose conflicts with the settlers are described by James H. O'Donnell III in *The Cherokees of North Carolina in the American Revolution* (Raleigh 1976), although I have not been able to find reliable descriptions of what they wore at the period.

40 'Donn' (brown-haired) is a term of endearment in Scottish Gaelic; he is presumably referring simply to the fishermen.

41 Gesto, one of the show-places of Skye, famed for a family of MacLeods to whom the *Gesto Collection of Highland Music*, ed K.N. MacDonald (Leipzig 1895), was dedicated.

42 This might refer to the massacre, with splitting of heads, which occurred at McLendon's Creek, following the wanton murder of a young boy by a British solider, ca 1776.

43 A mountain west of the Kintail Forest

44 'Marlin' probably refers to the loosely twisted tarred line, which may have been used for fishing in North Carolina at that time; it may refer to the tapering marlinspike. There is also a kind of oceanic sport fish known as marlin, but that cannot be what is meant here.

45 In Celtic tradition disloyalty to the king was considered a sure omen of bad luck and disaster.

46 Glen Shiel is a long glen south of the Kintail Forest.

Chapter 2: Nova Scotia

MICHAEL MACDONALD

1 In 1892 several articles were published in *The Casket* (31 March, 7 April, 1 September, all first-page columns), under the title 'Light and Shadows'; each of these gives information about this bard. See also brief notes in *MT* III, 6 (1895), 6: *Gaelic Bards* (1765-1825), 9; the Reverend John MacMillan, *The Early History of the Catholic Church in Prince Edward Island* (Quebec 1905), 181.

2 Captain John MacDonald of

Glenaladale sold his estate in Scotland and brought about 200 settlers, mostly from South Uist, to Prince Edward Island in 1772. It is well known that Catholic tenants in South Uist suffered great hardship and religious persecution at the hands of the Laird of Boisdale, and that Captain John's expedition was undertaken to relieve them. Recent studies on the subject are: Ian R. MacKay, 'Glenalladale's Settlement, Prince Edward Island,' *SGS* x (1963), 16-24; Reverend Allan F. MacDonald, 'Captain John MacDonald, "Glenalladale,"' *The Canadian Catholic Historical Association Report* xxxi (1964), 21-49.

3 *Casket* (7 April 1892), 1
4 MacMillan, *The Catholic Church*, 181
5 The author of 'Lights and Shadows,' n 1 above; his exact identity is unknown.
6 See Charles W. Dunn, *Highland Settler: A Portrait of the Scottish Gael in Nova Scotia* (Toronto 1953), 33; also *Lord Selkirk's Diary 1803-1804*, ed P.C.T. White (Toronto 1958), 8. General dissatisfaction with Glenaladale's terms may be accepted as the principal explanation for the large numbers of Highland emigrants who touched down on Prince Edward Island and shortly afterwards crossed over to Pictou, Antigonish, and Cape Breton, in the early nineteenth century. I am indebted to the late Father Anthony A. Johnson, Archivist for the Diocese of Antigonish, for further confirmation of this view, based on his extensive study of the letters and records of Bishop Angus B. MacEachern in foreign and local archives.

7 See John L. MacDougall, *History of Inverness County, Nova Scotia* (ca 1926), 189-90.
8 MacDougall, *History*, 190; *Gaelic Bards 1765-1825*, 9
9 MacMillan, *The Catholic Church*, 181
10 Local tradition known to the author of 'Lights and Shadows,' n 4 above.
11 *MT* III, 36 (1895), 6; *Collection of Folksongs and Music*, no 133
12 Texts: *MT* III, 50 (1895), 8; *Gaelic Bards 1765-1825*, 9-10; *Casket* (11 September 1930), 8. The Gaelic editor of *The Casket* appended a stanza he had heard from his mother, which is not entirely consistent with what is otherwise known about the bard and

his peregrinations. The stanza is as follows:

Gur mise bha gu brònach
'N uair thàinig mi 'n Bhras d'Or,
'Us 'n uair dh'fhàg mi 'n
    còmhlan
A bha thall, a bha thall, O.
Ach a nis 's ann leam nach misde;
Fhuair mi slios air am bheil fios
    'm
Nach dean idir, tha mi fiosrach,
Bonn a chall, bonn a chall.

I was very sad
when I came to Bras d'Or,
and when I left the company
who were over there.
But now I am none the worse for
    it;
I have property which I know,
without a doubt, will not
be unprofitable.

13 Literally 'bread'; 'talamh an arain,' 'bread land.' Cf 'ar,' 'ploughing' in Father Allan MacDonald, *Gaelic Words and Expressions from South Uist*, ed John Lorne Campbell Dublin 1958), 31.

14 Refers to the bard's brother who would not come with him to America; note in *MT* III, 50 (1895), 8.

15 This is the only reference to the feast of St Michael in all the songs of the emigrants examined for this collection. It is fitting that it should be made by a Hebridean. Traditional St Michael's day festivities were still current on South Uist and Canna in the late eighteenth century. This particular reference appears to recall the cause of religious oppression in South Uist. According to one tradition, the laird of Boisdale forbade his tenants to attend mass on the feast of St Michael, some years prior to their emigration to Prince Edward Island. The services of the tenants were required for the harvest. On the following Sunday, when the laird himself attended mass, he was publicly reprimanded by the priest, Father Wynn. Boisdale was incensed over this humiliation and soon afterwards initiated the anti-Catholic policy for which he is remembered. This note was contributed to *Am Mosgladh* I, 3 (1923), 43. The final stanza above is from oral recitation by A.A. Beaton, on 2 September 1973. It differs considerably from the published versions.

Mr Beaton, a former resident of St Ninian, Inverness County, Nova Scotia, described 'beice' (l 31) as a sign of recognition common in

Catholic Scotland in penal times. It was a gesture made with the feet, a quick shuffle, by which a priest was made aware of the identity of his fellow Catholics. The tradition lingered among emigrants in Nova Scotia. Mr Beaton recalled a specific instance in 1903 when one of his neighbours greeted a Highland priest with the 'beice,' and the greeting was duly acknowledged. Mr Beaton's rendering of line 30 was unintelligible.

FEAR A' MHUINNTIR MHEINNE

1 *TGSI* x (1881-3), 224
2 The disruption caused by the introduction of sheep into Strathglass is the subject of a very long song composed by Duncan Chisholm after he had emigrated to Nova Scotia, ca 1803; the text is in *CM* x (1885), 344-6, and *TGSI* xi (1884-5), 221-5. Telford noted in his *Report* (p 15) that the differences in rents to the landlords between sheep and cattle was at least three to one. Ultimately sheep would be numerous, he thought, but both sheep and cattle could be raised in the Highlands, and thus a substantial population could be supported.

3 Telford, *Report*, Appendix (c), 40-1: In 1801 the *Dove of Aberdeen* landed at Pictou and in 1802 the *Neptune*, with 550 emigrants destined for Upper Canada.
4 Text: *TGSI* x (1881-3), 224. Mary Chisholm married Seumas Gooden, a well-to-do merchant, and lived in London most of her life.

DONALD CHISHOLM

1 According to tradition, Donald Chisholm was tenth in lineal descent from John Farquharson of Braemar, a blacksmith, who had settled in Strathglass and was the progenitor of the Chisholms; see *Gaelic Bards 1765-1825*, 6. See also Alexander MacKenzie, *History of the Chisholms* (Inverness 1891), for references to the first great evictions from Strathglass in 1801, and *The Casket* (17 March 1892), 2, for the date of the bard's arrival in Nova Scotia.
2 *TGSI* x (1881-3), 225
3 Texts: *TGSI* x (1881-3), 227-8; *MT* iii, 50 (1895), 8, used here
4 *'N uair theid Flòri 'na h-éideadh* (*When Flòri is rigged*); Text: *TGSI* x (1881-3), 229; text and translation are below, pp. 00-00.

5 *Casket* (17 March 1892), 2
6 Father William is known to
have served for a number of
years in the diocese of Antigonish, after receiving part of
his education in Baltimore,
Maryland; the Reverend A.A.
Johnson, *History of the
Catholic Church in Eastern
Nova Scotia* I (Antigonish
1961), 380. Donald Og settled
in Cape Breton, but he was
never happy there as may be
inferred from his song, *Ach
na'm bithinn òg* (*If I were
young*), TGSI x (1881-3), 230.
Archibald and John took up
residence at Margaree Forks
(ca 1809), and opened a
blacksmith shop there.
7 A manuscript history of
Donald Gobha's family was
in possession of one of his
descendants at Antigonish
Harbour in 1929. It was used
by Reverend D.J. Rankin
when he compiled his *History
of Antigonish County* (Antigonish 1929); see p 84.
8 This probably means that he
will retreat from the evictions
being carried out by his landlord.
9 Meaning not clear; it may
refer to religious differences
between east and west or to
some other divisive force
known to the bard.
10 There is an island by this

name six miles southwest of
Beauly, at the mouth of a
river which empties from
Glen Affric.

JOHN MACLEAN

1 Except where otherwise
stated, the following account
is based on the biographical
sketch of John Maclean given
by the Reverend Alexander
Maclean Sinclair (grandson
of the bard) in *Filidh na
Coille*, 8-16, and in *Clarsach*,
xiv-xxi.
2 Bard Maclean had two rare
manuscript volumes of Gaelic
poetry: a collection made by
Hector MacLean of Tober-
mory in 1768, seen by Johnson during his tour of the
Islands in 1773, and the
other, a collection of Gaelic
songs and classical poetry
which he had made himself
before he emigrated. Thanks
to the bard's descendants,
both manuscripts are now in
the Public Archives of Nova
Scotia.
3 Only Gaelic speakers could
attend the ball. The bard
honoured the occasion with
this song and its familiar refrain:

Bithibh aotrom 's togaibh fonn,
Cridheil, sunndach gun bhith
    trom,

'G òl deoch-slàinte na bheil
    thall
Ann an tìr nam beann 's nan
    gleannaibh.

Be light of heart and sing
merrily with spirits high,
as we drink to the health of all
    those
we left in the land of the bens and
    glens.
(*Filidh na Coille*, 66-8)

4 Texts: *Clarsach*, 88-90; the
editor states that he obtained
part of this song while on a
visit to Tiree in 1869 and the
rest of it later from Duncan
Cameron, Caledonia, Nova
Scotia. The text is also printed
in *Filidh na Coille*, 47-8.

5 Texts: *Clarsach*, 142-5; *Filidh
na Coille*, 104-7; partial text
in *The Tiree Bards*, ed Reverend Hector Cameron (Stirling
1932), 91-2. *Cuairtear nan
Gleann* (Tourist of the Glens)
was a popular Gaelic periodical, which enjoyed a wide
circulation in the Highlands
and in Gaelic communities
overseas. Its editor, the Reverend Norman MacLeod, was
a master of Gaelic idiom, and
many of the interesting items
in the *Cuairtear* were from his
own hand. Bard Maclean
composed this song to wel-
come the periodical to America about 1842.

6 Colonel Simon Fraser had induced the bard to emigrate
and assured him that those
who had gone before him
were now enjoying untold
prosperity; see *Seann Albainn
agus Albainn Ur* (*Old and New
Scotland*), a song in which the
bard represents a debate
between himself and the
colonel on the subject of emigration, in *Clarsach*, 94-100.

7 Although this phrase is not
entirely clear, this seems to
be the correct rendering.

8 John the Miller Sutherland
was one of the victims of the
Sutherland evictions carried
out by the notorious Patrick
Sellar. He had served for
many years as forester for the
earl of Sutherland before he
came to Barney's River in
1821. He died in March 1840,
at the age of 105. The last line
of this quatrain alludes to the
fact that he always wore his
kilt; see *Clarsach*, 145.

9 *Cuairtear nan Gleann* succeeded *Teachdaire Ur Gaelach*
('The New Highland Cou-
rier'), 1835-6, which had
succeeded *Teachdaire Gaelach*
('Highland Courier'), 1829-
31. All three were edited by
the Reverend Norman Mac-
Leod and published in Glasgow.

10 According to a note in *Clar-*

sach (p 145) the person
referred to as proving that
Gaelic was the language of
Adam and Eve is Lachlan
MacLean of Coll, author of
the *History of the Celtic Language*, and other works.

JOHN MACDONALD

1 Brief notices about John the
Hunter MacDonald are given
in unpublished manuscripts
of Allan MacDonald (the
Ridge), undated, originals in
the Special Collections of St
Francis Xavier University,
Antigonish. See also *MT* XI,
24 (1903), 192: *Guth na Bliadhna*, I, 3 (1904), 250-4; *Casket* (8 May 1930), 8 and (21
August 1930), 8; the Reverend Alexander D. MacDon-
ald, *Mabou Pioneers* (privately
printed, ca 1962), 581.
2 Texts: *MT* XI 24 (1903), 192,
used here with the two final
stanzas added from the *Casket* (13 March 1930), 8; Ridge
mss, np; *Fàilte Cheap Breatuin*, ed James H. McNeil
(typescript, Sydney 1933),
85-7.
3 In another song composed
about 1840 the bard speaks of
how rapidly his savings
dwindled after he emigrated;
Casket (7 April 1932), 8.
4 It was an ancient tradition

that the MacDonalds were
always first in rank among
the clans in battle.
5 14 September, feast of the
exaltation of the Holy Cross.
6 The bard's disdain for those
around him on Mabou Ridge
suggests that he considered
himself superior to them.
This line may mean that he
regrets being reduced to a
lower social class than that to
which he belonged in Lochaber.
7 The churchyard of St Cairrail, in the Braes of Lochaber,
is a very ancient site. The
church was restored in 1932
with the help of friends from
Mabou, Nova Scotia, many of
whose ancestors are buried in
the churchyard. An interesting account of the restoration
ceremonies was published in
the *Oban Times* (30 July
1932).
8 Notably the celebrated bard
Iain Lom MacDonald, and
more recently Bishop Ken-
neth Grant, bishop of Argyle
and the Isles, who died in
1959.

ALLAN MACDONALD

1 Some information about this
bard is given in an article
written by his grand-
daughter, Mary A. MacDon-

ald, South River, Antigonish County, Nova Scotia (clipping attached to cover of one of the volumes of the Ridge mss). For other information see Keith N. MacDonald, *The MacDonald Bards from Medieval Times* (Glasgow 1900), 100-2.

2 Ridge mss (large volume), 192-3

3 Text: Ridge mss (large volume), 6-8

JOHN MACQUEEN

1 There are some discrepancies in the surviving fragmentary notes about this poet. The following account is a reconstruction based on notes in *MT* XII, 7 (1903), 56, a notice in *Guth na Bliadhna* IV (1907), 41-2; and remarks by Sorley MacLean in 'Poetry of the Clearances,' *TGSI* XXXVIII (1937-41), 310, who gives the bard's name as Donald and his place of residence as Totascore in Skye.

2 R. Fraser MacKenzie composed a song for 'Hattie Og' when she went to Nova Scotia some time in the nineteenth century; *MT* V, 24 (1895), 8. A similar song by Alan Livingstone, composed for Mary Maclean, another

emigrant, was published in *An t-Oranaiche*, ed Archibald Sinclair (Glasgow 1879), 17-19. Songs of women bereft of their suitors may be noted, too; eg, *Tha e nis air falbh uam* (*He is now gone from me*), by Lady D'oyly in *An t-Oranaiche*, 281-3, and *MT* X, 23 (1902), 175. *Gun Crodh Gun Aighean* (*Without cows or chattels*) is the best known of this class. The genre is well known in the Irish tradition and may be traced to continental themes of a much earlier period. Several songs of the kind are included in *Songs of the Irish*, ed Donald O'Sullivan (New York 1960).

3 Texts: *MT* XII, 7 (1903), 56. The song is also to be found in many collections of Gaelic songs.

KENNETH MACDONALD

1 The only reference to this bard is the note in *MT* IX, 29 (1901), 224. He is not mentioned in *MacDonald Bards* or in any of the collections of the Reverend A. Maclean Sinclair.

2 I have not seen any other emigrant song from that area relating to the early nineteenth century. It is reason-

able to assume that there are many more, although as yet (to my knowledge) unpublished. *Oran do America* is included here principally because it is representative of a significant Highland settlement in eastern Cape Breton Island.

3 Text: *MT* IX, 29 (1901), 224

DUNCAN BLACK BLAIR

1 Biographical data on Dr Blair are based on A. Maclean Sinclair, 'The Reverend Dr. Blair's Manuscripts,' *Celtic Review* II (1906), 153-60, and *Gaelic Bards 1825-75*, 139-40, and 152. See also the Reverend George Patterson, *A History of Pictou County* (Montreal 1877), 429, where the author states that after the disruption of the Church of Scotland in 1846 the people of Blue Mountain and Barney's River joined the Free Church and obtained Dr Blair as their first minister in 1848.

2 Texts: *MT* XII, 10 (1903), 79; *Gaelic Bards 1825-75*, 106-7

3 Loch Brura is about ten miles east of Blue Mountain.

Chapter 3: Prince Edward Island

CALUM BÀN MACMHANNAIN

1 The few details known about this bard are given in *MT* XI, 10 (1902), 79, and in *Gaelic Bards 1765-1825*, 80. Inquiries addressed to scholars in Scotland, Charlottetown, and Antigonish, failed to elicit any additional information. I am indebted to the Reverend William Matheson for the following note concerning the name MacMhannain: 'This surname should really be spelled *Mac Bhannain*. In sixteenth century records referring to Skye it appears as "mc banane," and it may be the same name as Irish Bannon. In Skye (and also in Lewis) it is now anglicised, but misleadingly, as Buchanan. They were once an influential tribe in Arran, but their history is quite obscure.'

2 Texts: *MT* III, 41 (1895), 9; *MT* XI, 10 (1902), 79; *Gaelic Bards 1765-1825*, 81-5. The song is also on tape in the Archives of the School of Scottish Studies, University of Edinburgh, recorded from the Reverend Norman MacDonald (cat. no. SA 53 Skye).

3 Using the Ordnance Survey

maps I have been able to identify the following places in Skye referred to in the song: Rona, an island northeast of Portree; Digg, in Kilmuir; Eilean Trodday, off the northeast tip of Skye; Clach nan Ramh, a small reef off Flodigarry; Bodha Ruadh, a submerged rock on the southside of Kilmaluag Bay; Rubha na h-Aiseig, northeast of the Aird, opposite Trodday; Rubha Hunish, promontory off the northwest coast of Skye, two miles north of Duntulm; Fladda-Chuain, near Kilmuir; Rubh' a'Chairn Leith, west of Kilmuir; Storr, a prominent height of land, the Storr (2358') above the 'Old Man of Storr'; Rigg, a grazing ground now deserted; Carn, Carn Liath, an area adjacent to Rigg, also used for grazing, probably the north shoulder of the Storr; Grobainn, 'The Knoll,' outer end of a long peninsula between Loch Fallort and Davoch Bay, north of Sarsdal.

4 This place name may have some reference to the flagstone for the drop of milk poured to propitiate the 'gruagach' (long-haired one). Interesting notes about this spirit are given by the Reverend Cyril H. Dieckhoff in 'Mythological Beings in Gaelic Folklore,' *TGSI* XXIX (1914-19), 235-58.

5 The identity of this particular vulture and his predecessor is not clear.

6 Campbells were prominent as factors in Assynt in the latter part of the eighteenth century. Possibly this is a reference to a later member of the clan exercising that function.

7 Probably the second Lord MacDonald who succeeded the unpopular Sir Alexander, under whom Skye had witnessed massive emigration at the end of the eighteenth century.

RORY ROY MACKENZIE

1 Rory Roy's association with the earl of Selkirk is established in the first line of his song *An Imrich* (*The Emigration*). He is mentioned in Selkirk's *Diary* (p 15 and p 30), where the earl describes him as a principal man among the colonists from Ross-shire, one of the two who were 'more gentlemen than the rest of the Settlers.' I am in-

debted to Dr J.M. Bumsted, Simon Fraser University, and to Mrs J.B. Barrett, Charlotte-town, a direct descendant of Rory Roy, for biographical data to supplement the fragmentary details in *MT* III, 36 (1895), 6; *TGSI* XII (1885-6), 118-19; *Mac-Talla Nan Tur*, 126; and *Gaelic Bards 1765-1825*, 77.

2 Information from Dr Bumsted: Selkirk Papers, volume 56, 14862-69

3 Biographical data provided by Mrs Barrett with transcripts from the Public Records of Nova Scotia and reference from deeds registered in the Prince Edward Island Land Office.

4 Texts: *MT* III, 36 (1895), 6; *Gaelic Bards 1765-1825*, 78-80, is used here because it is the more complete.

5 St Mary's Isle in Kirkcudbrightshire was the seat of the Selkirk estate.

6 Dr Angus Macaulay was appointed one of Selkirk's agents in 1803. He emigrated to Prince Edward Island and received a grant of land in the Point Prim district. He was an active and respected member of the pioneer community. Selkirk makes fre-

quent references to him in his *Diary*.

A MACLEAN BARD FROM RAASAY

1 Text of song and introduction: *MT* VII, 11 (1898), 87; ll 29-30 are missing.

2 Eighty-four families of Highlanders arrived at Charlottetown on 1 June 1829 and later proceeded to Murray Harbour; see Malcolm A. Mac-Queen, *Skye Pioneers and 'the Island'* (Winnipeg 1929), 72. Settlers from Raasay came to various parts of the Island in 1828, 1830, 1834, and 1840; Malcolm Lamond, 'Na h-Eilthirich' (The Emigrants), *MT* III, 5 (1894), 6-7.

IAIN SINCLAIR

1 For information about this bard see *Gaelic Bards 1825-75*, 138, and *An Gàidheal* III (1874), 19.

2 Published in *An Gàidheal* III (1874), 217-18; *MT* XI, 1 (1902), 7, and XII, 6 (1903), 7, and in several later publications.

3 Texts: *An Gàidheal* III (1874), 19-20; *MT* XII, 7 (1903), 56. The latter has been used here. The title is one of two given

by the editor of *An Gàidheal*;
in the *MT* edition the song is
entitled *An Comunn Comhal-
lach*.

Chapter 4: Ontario

ANNA GILLIS

1 Brief references to Anna Gillis are given by Conal in the
   Casket (7 September 1893), 4,
   and in *Gaelic Bards 1825-75*,
   6; see also comments in
   Gairm XII (1955), 324. For the
   arrival of the *MacDonald* at
   Quebec, see J.A. MacDonell,
   *Sketches illustrating the Early
   Settlement and History of Glengarry, Canada* (Montreal
   1893). Her name is variously
   spelt: Gillies, McGillies, Gillis.
2 Of the many accounts of
   early settlement in Glengarry
   some of the most useful are:
   MacDonell, *Sketches*; Edwin
   C. Guillet, *Early Life in Upper
   Canada* (Toronto 1933),
   35-47; A. Maclean Sinclair,
   'Gàidheil Ghlinnegaradh an
   Ontario' (Glengarry Highlanders in Ontario), *MT* IV,
   43 (1896), 2-3. A letter written from Chambly, Canada,
   26 December 1814, in *Family
   Memoir of the MacDonalds of*

Keppoch, ed Clemens R.
Markham (London 1885),
145-59, provides an interesting picture of the Highland
settlement in Glengarry and
nearby Stormont. Cultural
aspects of the settlement are
dealt with by Charles W.
Dunn in 'Glengarry's Gaelic
Heritage,' *Dalhousie Review*
XLII (1962-3), 196-201.
3 Guillet, *Early Life*, p. 41. This
   assumption is based in part
   on a tentative deduction:
   Reverend John MacDonald,
   his brother Aeneas, and his
   sister, Sister St Pelagie of the
   Congregation de Notre Dame,
   Montreal, were children of
   John MacDonald and Anna
   McGillies, emigrants from
   Scotland. Sister St Pelagie was
   baptized at St Andrew's,
   County Stormont, 12 March
   1790 (CND Archives, Montreal). The parish was probably under the ministry of
   Father Alexander (Scotus)
   MacDonell; Catholics in
   Glengarry and Stormont
   were under his jurisdiction.
4 *Casket* (7 September 1893), 4.
   Many of her relatives are said
   to have settled in Cape Breton.
5 J.G. Harkness, *Stormont, Dun-
   das and Glengarry* (Oshawa
   1946), 183. The fact that Sir

John was buried in the old cemetery at St Andrew's supports the assumption discussed above, n 3.

6 *Celtic Magazine*, V (1879), 159 and 235

7 Texts: *MT* XI, 19 (1903), 152; *Gaelic Bards 1825-75*, 6-7; *Gairm* XII (1955), 324-5, used here

8 Texts: *MT* XI, 9 (1903), 151; *Gaelic Bards 1825-75*, 7-8; *Casket* (7 September 1893), 4. The first four stanzas and the last edited below are from *MT*; lines 13-15 from the *Casket* have been substituted for a similar stanza in *MT* which does not specify that Father Alexander was of the house of Scotus. The reference distinguishes him from his namesake, the future bishop of Kingston, who brought other emigrants from Scotland to Glengarry in 1803.

9 Figures on the MacDonald arms. As early as 1471 the official arms of the Lord of the Isles consisted of three lions rampant, a lymphad or galley under sail, an eagle, a dexter hand issuing from the base holding a sword in bend sinister, all within a royal tressure; *The Scots Peerage* V (Edinburgh 1908), 48.

10 By 1814 every family had 200 acres according to *Family Memoir*, 146.

AN ANONYMOUS
GLENGARRY BARD

1 The song and the Gaelic introduction were recorded by Charles W. Dunn. There is a copy of the recording in the Celtic Archives, Boylston Hall, Harvard University, Scottish Gaelic Tape 7, # 78-89, Glengarry and Dalhousie Station.

2 A fellow emigrant with the bard, known locally as the 'Drover'; information from C.W. Dunn.

HUGH MACCORKINDALE

1 Text: *An Gaidheal* VI (1877), 42-3

2 Photo-copy from the Department of Public Records and Archives of Ontario, *Directory*, 218

3 Edited with translation by W.J. Watson in *Scottish Verse from the Book of the Dean of Lismore* (Edinburgh 1937), 60-5

Chapter 5: Manitoba and the North West Territories

DÒMHNALL DIOMBACH AND HIS COMPATRIOT

1 James N. MacKinnon, *A Short History of the Pioneer Scotch Settlers of St. Andrews, Sask* (1921), passim. I am indebted to Dr Margaret MacKay, School of Scottish Studies, University of Edinburgh, for this reference and for general information about Gaelic settlers in Wapella, Manitoba. The pipers named by MacKinnon were from Benbecula: Donald John McDonald, Donald McDonald, and Roderick MacIsaac. Ewen McKinnon, Ronald McCormick, and Angus McDougall are described as Gaelic storytellers.

2 MacKinnon, 18. The others were Mrs Farquhar Beaton (Christena McRury) and her son Norman.

3 For another ascription see Hugh MacPhee, 'The Trail of the Emigrants,' *TGSI* XLVI (1969-70), 214-15. A partial text of this song appeared in *MT* III, 31 (1895), 4. I am indebted to Mr Donald Meek, Department of Celtic Studies, University of Glasgow, for a copy of a complete transcription from *The Scottish Highlander* (28 February 1899). This transcription was made by Mr Hugh Barron, Gaelic Society of Inverness, who generously permitted me to use it in preference to the *MT* text. (I have made a few slight changes.) The text of *Freagradh do Dhòmhnall Diombach* (*Reply to Resentful Donald*) is from *MT* III, 32 (1895), 1.

4 See Norman MacDonald, *Canada, Immigration and Colonization 1841-1903* (Aberdeen 1966), 244. According to another authority, the CPR plan antedated Rankin's. Under the former, farms were offered to settlers for $2.50 an acre with a rebate of $1.25 for every acre broken and put to cultivation; *Canada and its Provinces*, XX, ed Adam Shortt and Arthur G. Doughty (Toronto 1914), 302.

5 MacDonald, *Immigration*, 194-5

6 Place unidentified; 'Bàigh' may be a mis-spelling for 'Braigh'; if so the English would read 'the Braes.'

7 Possibly a reference to one of Lady Gordon-Cathcart's agents

8 Lady Gordon-Cathcart, proprietor of Benbecula and Cluny

9 See MacKinnon, 12, where

one 'Domhnull Chalum' is identified as Donald Mac-Innes of Gerinish, South Uist, who emigrated to the North-west Territories in 1884.

10 Sir George Stephen

ANGUS MACINTOSH

1 Text with a bibliographical note in the *Celtic Monthly* XIII (1905), 78
2 It had been published earlier in *MT* XII, 23 (1904), 189.
3 The Allan Steamship Lines were, of course, famous propagandists for emigration, and in the nineteenth century their agents took a leading part in advertising Canada.
4 This may refer to the lands of the Qu'Appelle Land Com-pany or of the Saskatchewan Valley Land Company which displaced it in 1902. A suc-cession of companies engaged with varying degrees of suc-cess in opening up the Cana-dian west in the second half of the nineteenth century.

Chapter 6: The Tradition Adapted

1 Robert England discusses this movement with specific ref-erences to Scottish emigrants in his work, *The Colonization of Western Canada* (London 1936).
2 Text: *Tiree Bards*, 227-8
3 Text: *Casket* (9 July 1925), 2
4 Text: *Casket* (9 December 1926), 8
5 Text: *Mactalla Nan Tur*, 119-20
6 Text: *Fàilte Cheap Breatuin*, 69-70

Index of Proper Names

Index of Place Names

Glossarial Index

Each word in this index is identified by the number of the page, followed by the number of the line, on which it is first to be found.

This book

was designed by

WILLIAM RUETER

and was printed by

University of

Toronto

Press